COLLECT THE SET!

Boffin Boy and the Invaders from Space
978 184167 613 5

Boffin Boy and the Wizard of Edo
978 184167 614 2

Boffin Boy and the Monsters from the Deep
978 184167 615 9

Boffin Boy and the Red Wolf
978 184167 616 6

Boffin Boy and the Lost City
978 184167 617 3

Boffin Boy and the Time Warriors
978 184167 622 7

Boffin Boy and the Ice Caves of Pluto
978 184167 626 5

Boffin Boy and the Quest for Wisdom
978 184167 628 9

Boffin Boy and the Deadly Swarm
978 184167 625 8

Boffin Boy and the Rock Men
978 184167 624 1

Boffin Boy and the Temples of Mars
978 184167 623 4

Boffin Boy and the Forest of the Ninja
978 184167 627 2

Boffin Boy and the Deadly Swarm
by David Orme

Illustrated by Peter Richardson

Published by Ransom Publishing Ltd.
51 Southgate Street, Winchester, Hants. SO23 9EH
www.ransom.co.uk

ISBN   978 184167 625 8
First published in 2007
Second printing 2008
Copyright © 2007 Ransom Publishing Ltd.

Illustrations copyright © 2007 Peter Richardson

Design & layout: *www.macwiz.co.uk*
Printed in China through Colorcraft Ltd., Hong Kong.

Find out more about Boffin Boy at *www.ransom.co.uk.*

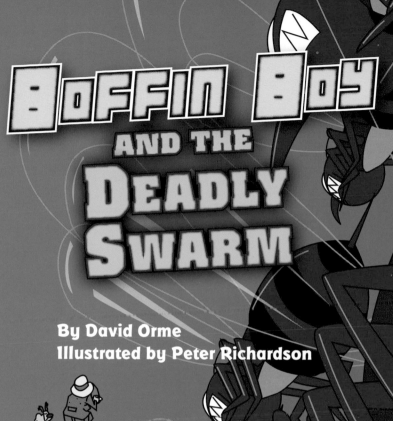

Boffin Boy
AND THE
Deadly
Swarm

By David Orme
Illustrated by Peter Richardson

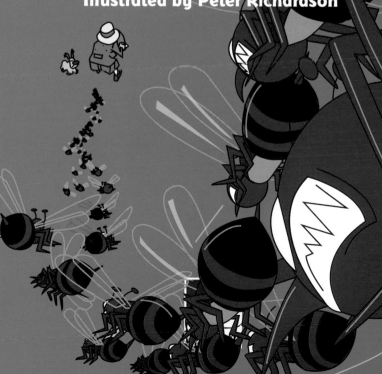

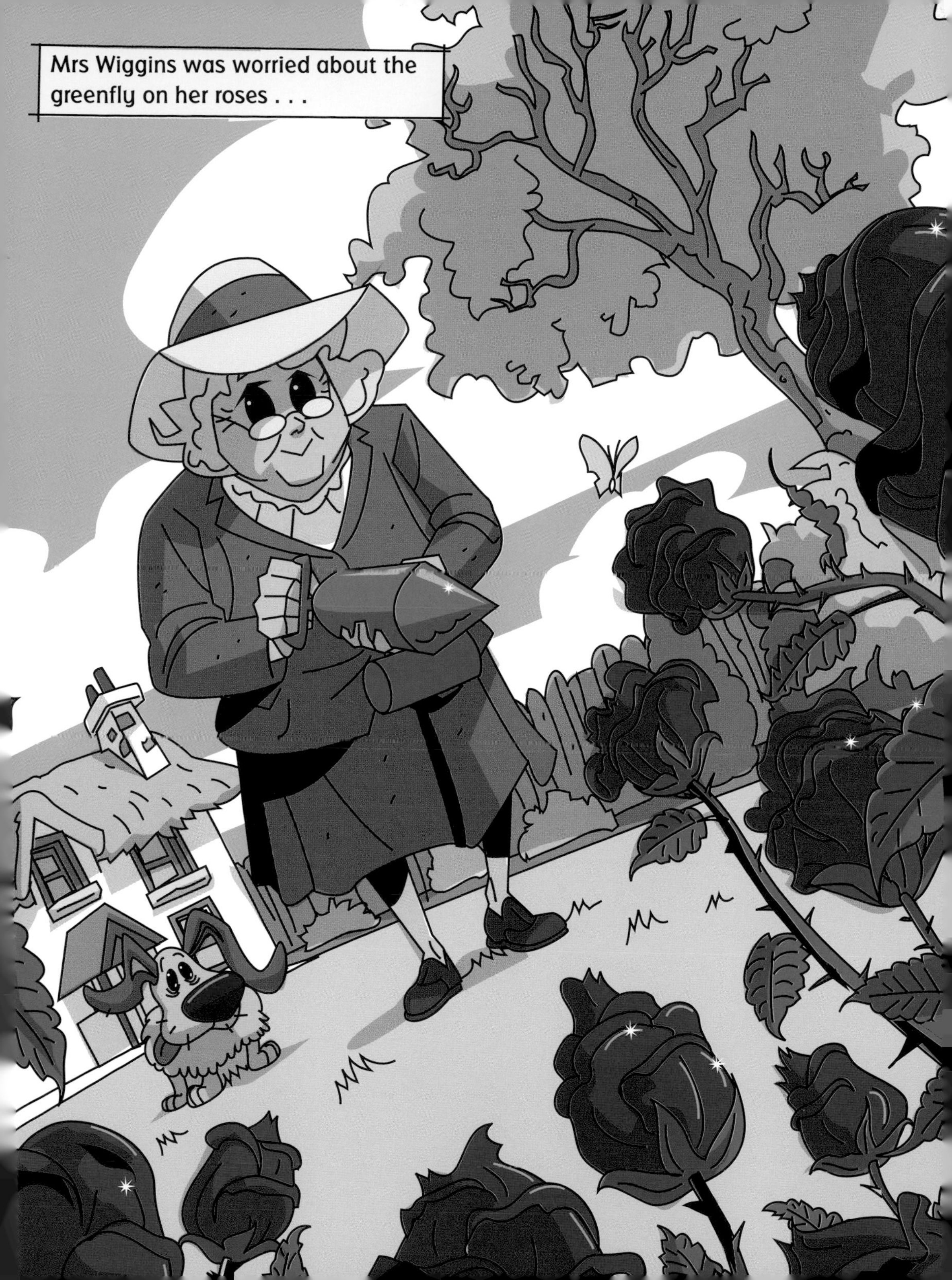
Mrs Wiggins was worried about the greenfly on her roses . . .

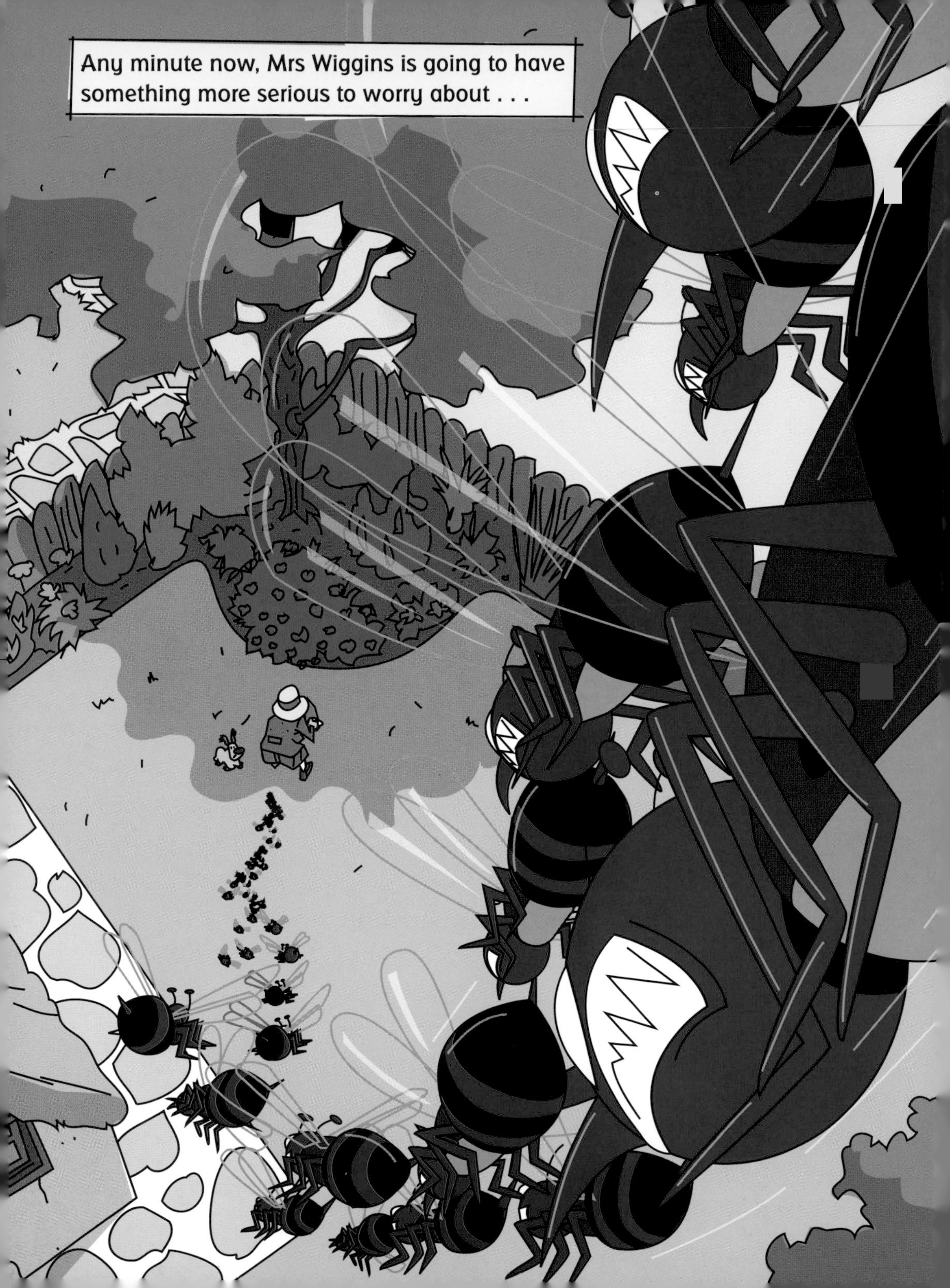
Any minute now, Mrs Wiggins is going to have something more serious to worry about . . .

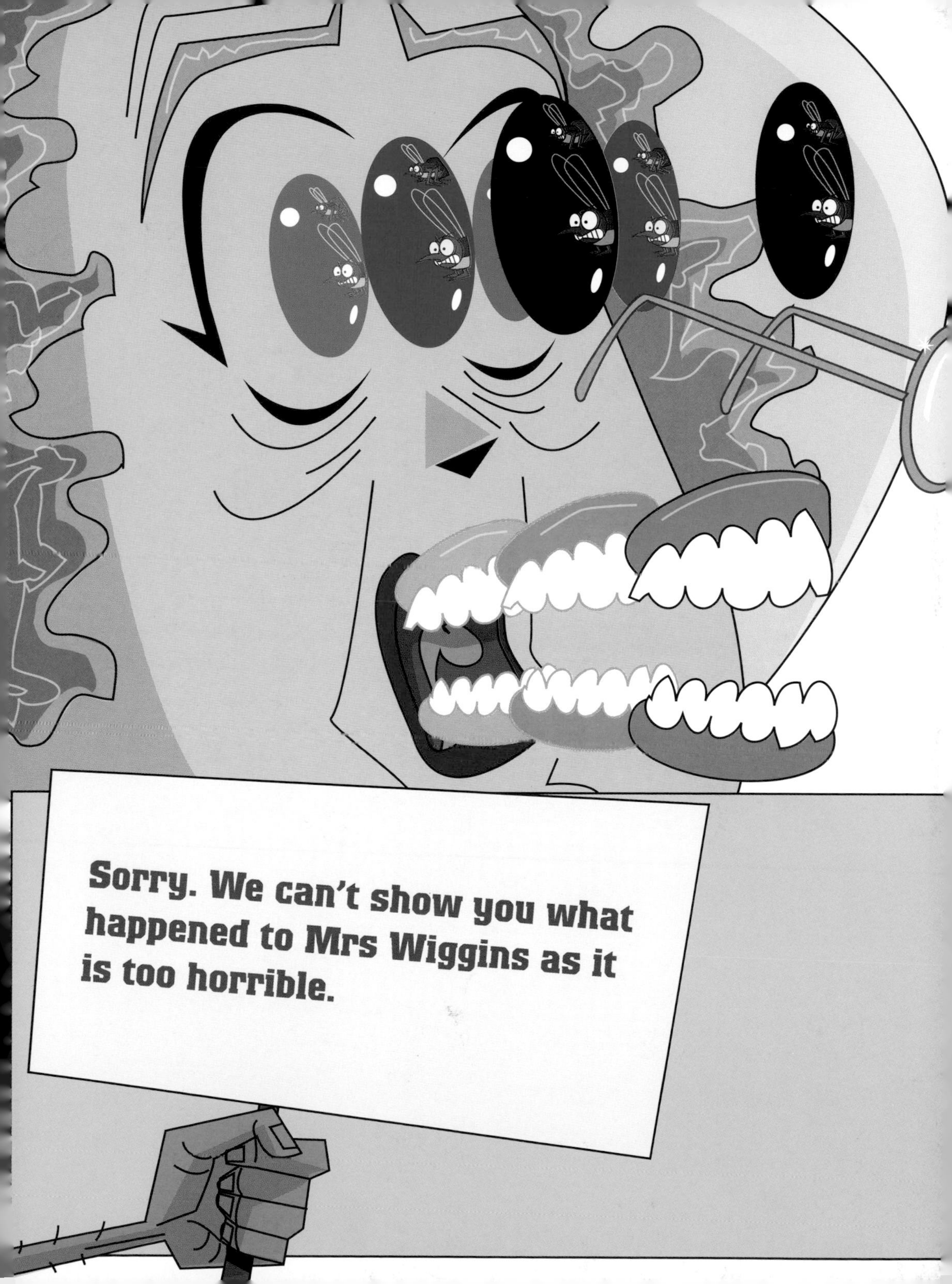
Sorry. We can't show you what happened to Mrs Wiggins as it is too horrible.

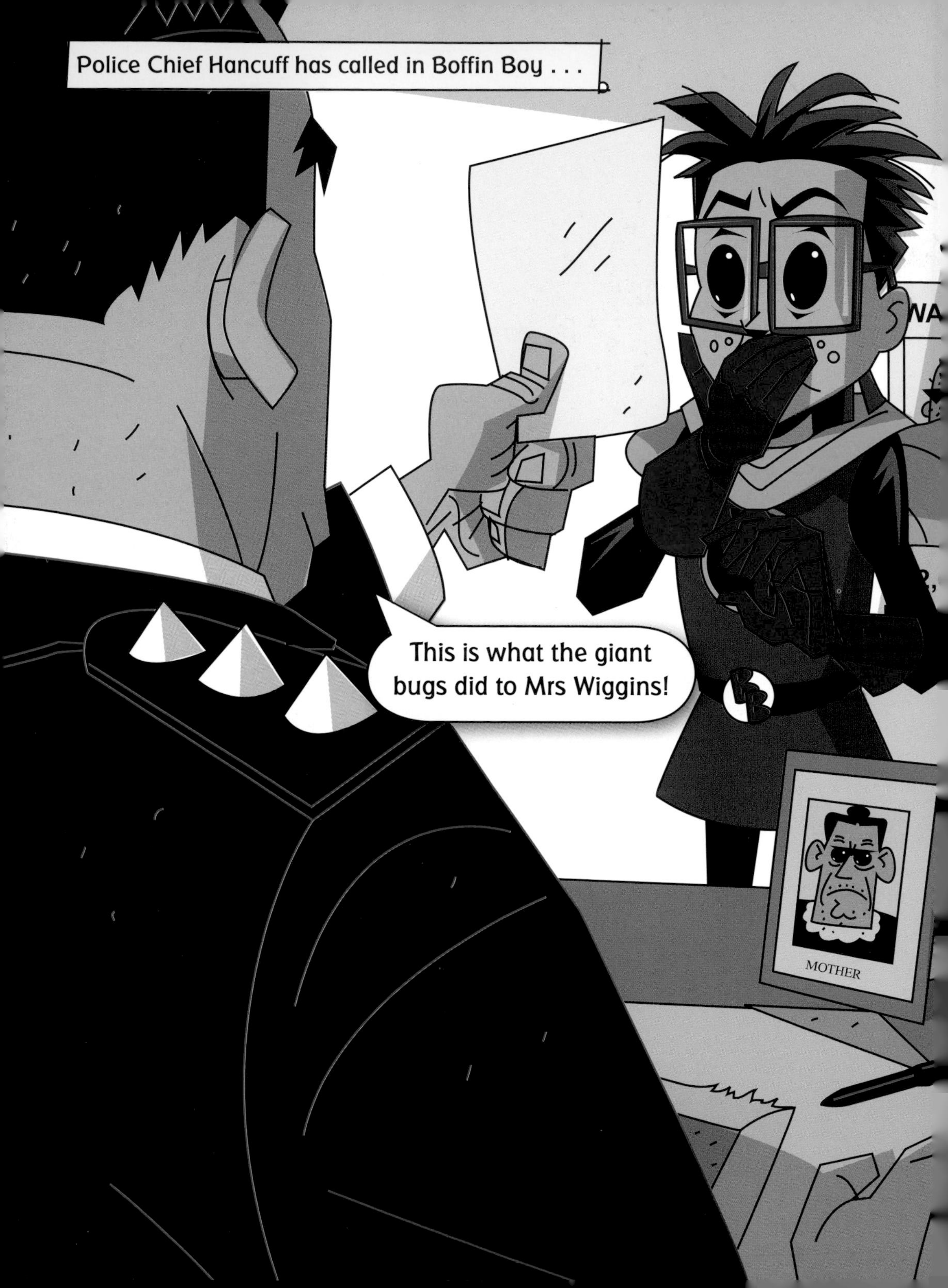
Police Chief Hancuff has called in Boffin Boy . . .
This is what the giant bugs did to Mrs Wiggins!
MOTHER

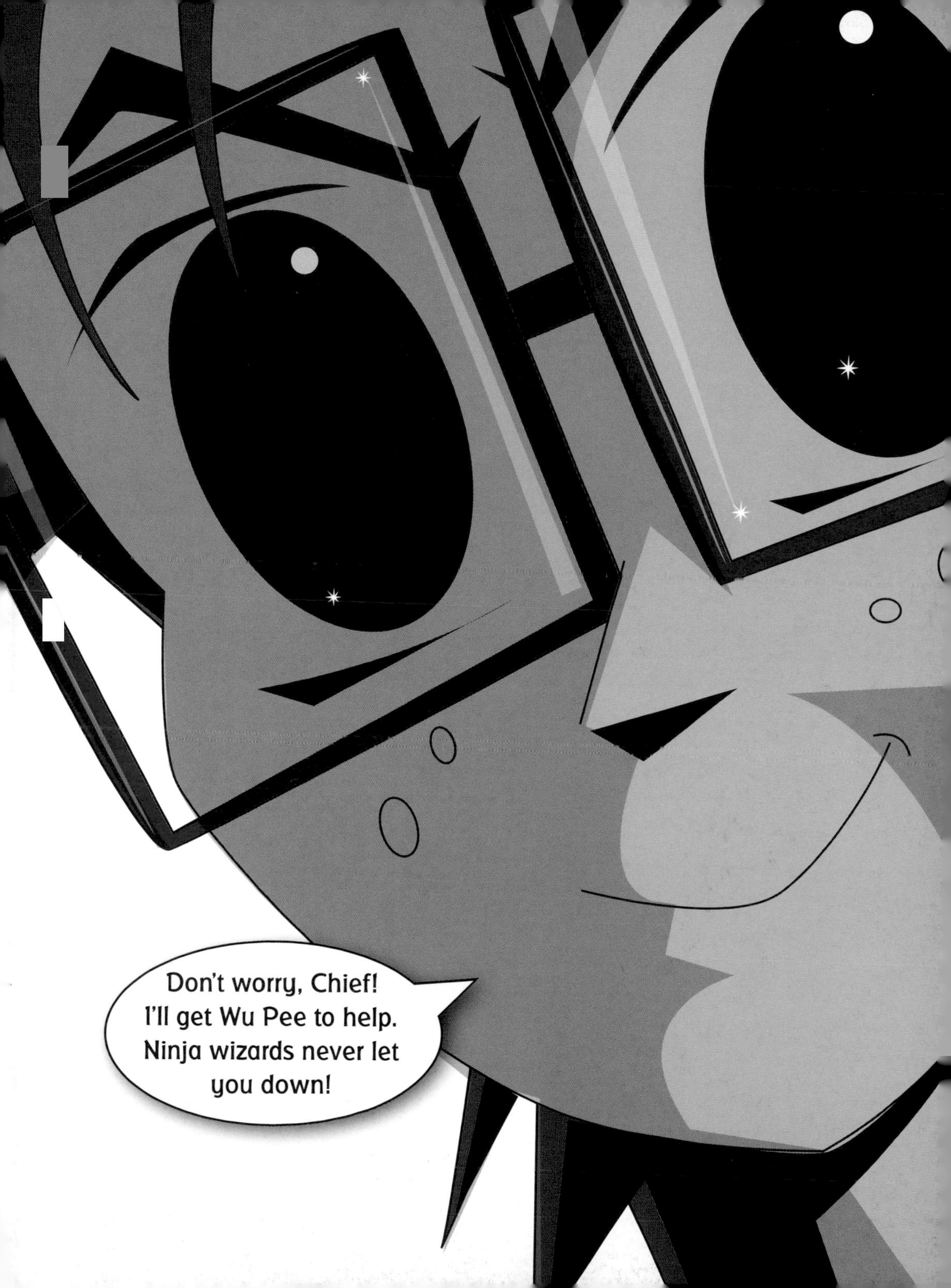
Don't worry, Chief! I'll get Wu Pee to help. Ninja wizards never let you down!

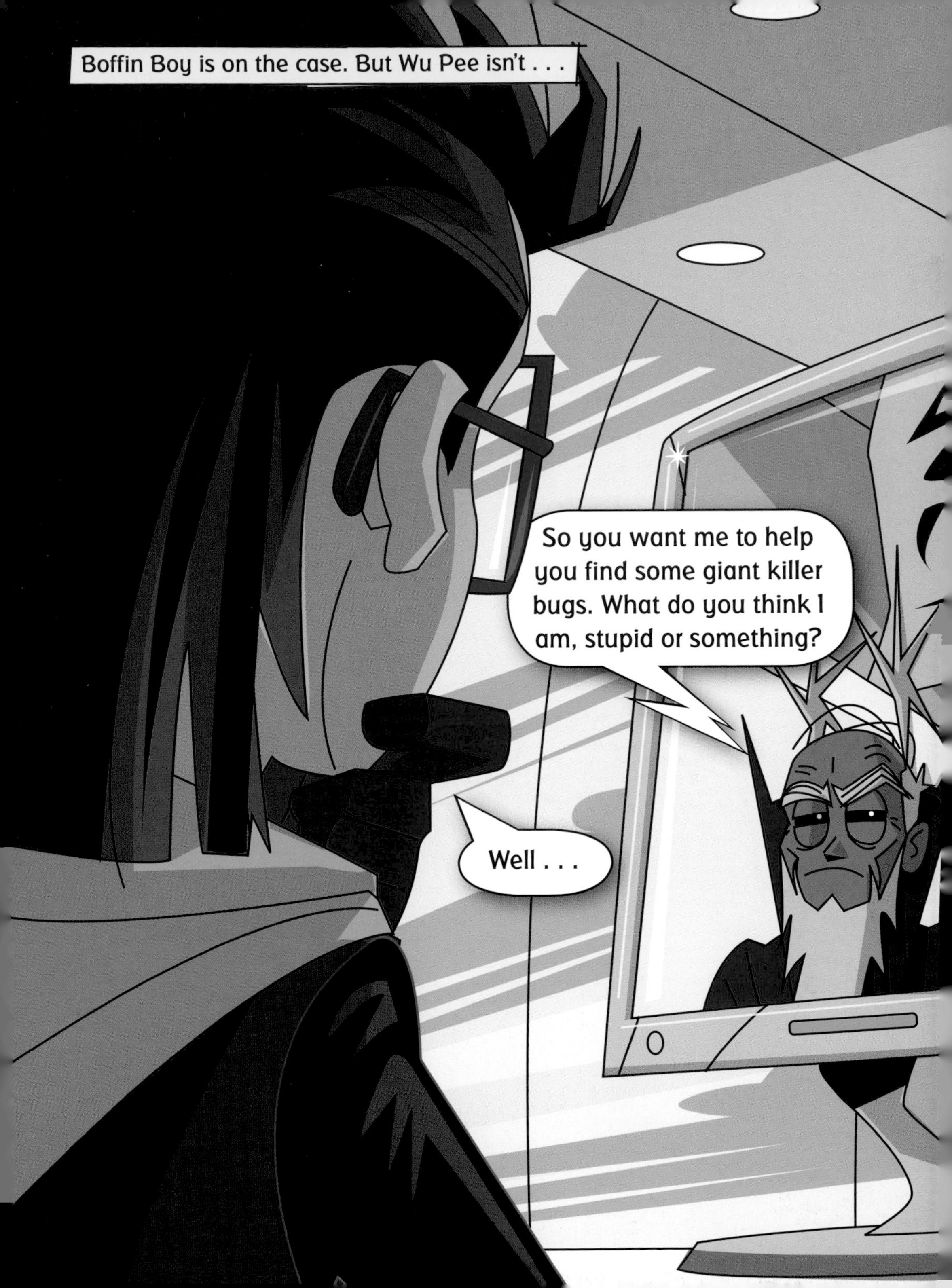
Boffin Boy is on the case. But Wu Pee isn't . . .
So you want me to help you find some giant killer bugs. What do you think I am, stupid or something?
Well . . .

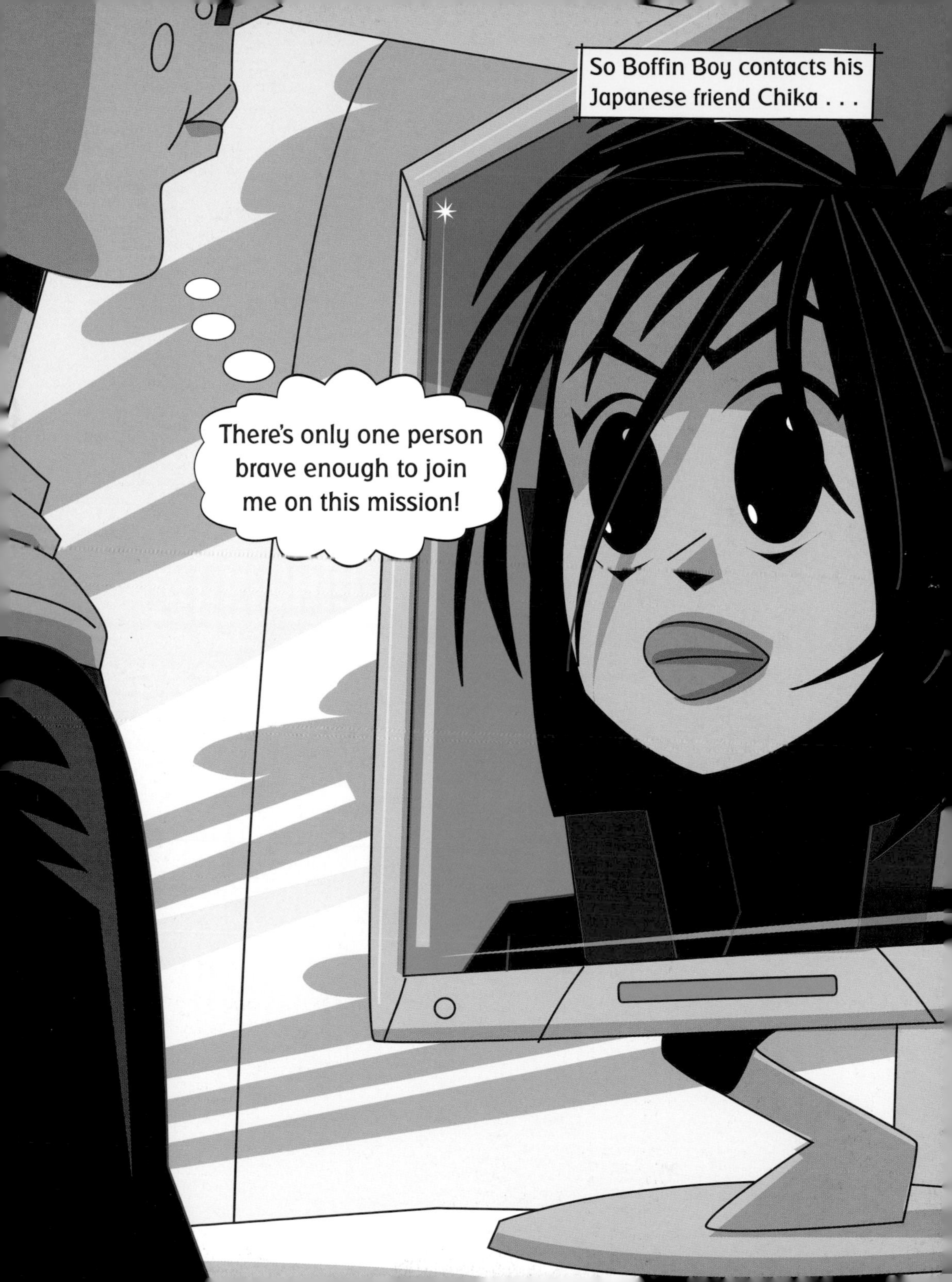
So Boffin Boy contacts his Japanese friend Chika . . .
There's only one person brave enough to join me on this mission!

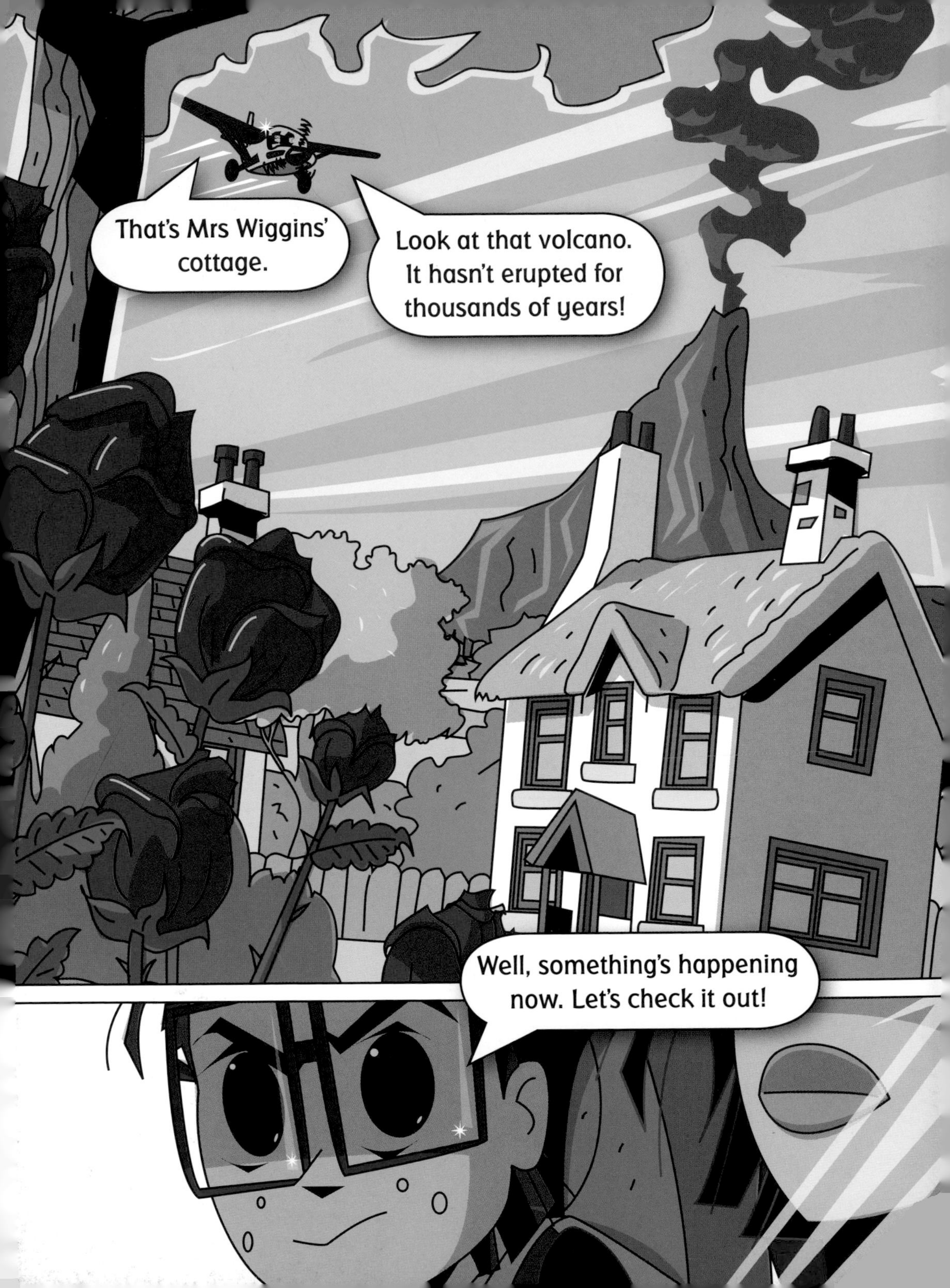
That's Mrs Wiggins' cottage.
Look at that volcano. It hasn't erupted for thousands of years!
Well, something's happening now. Let's check it out!

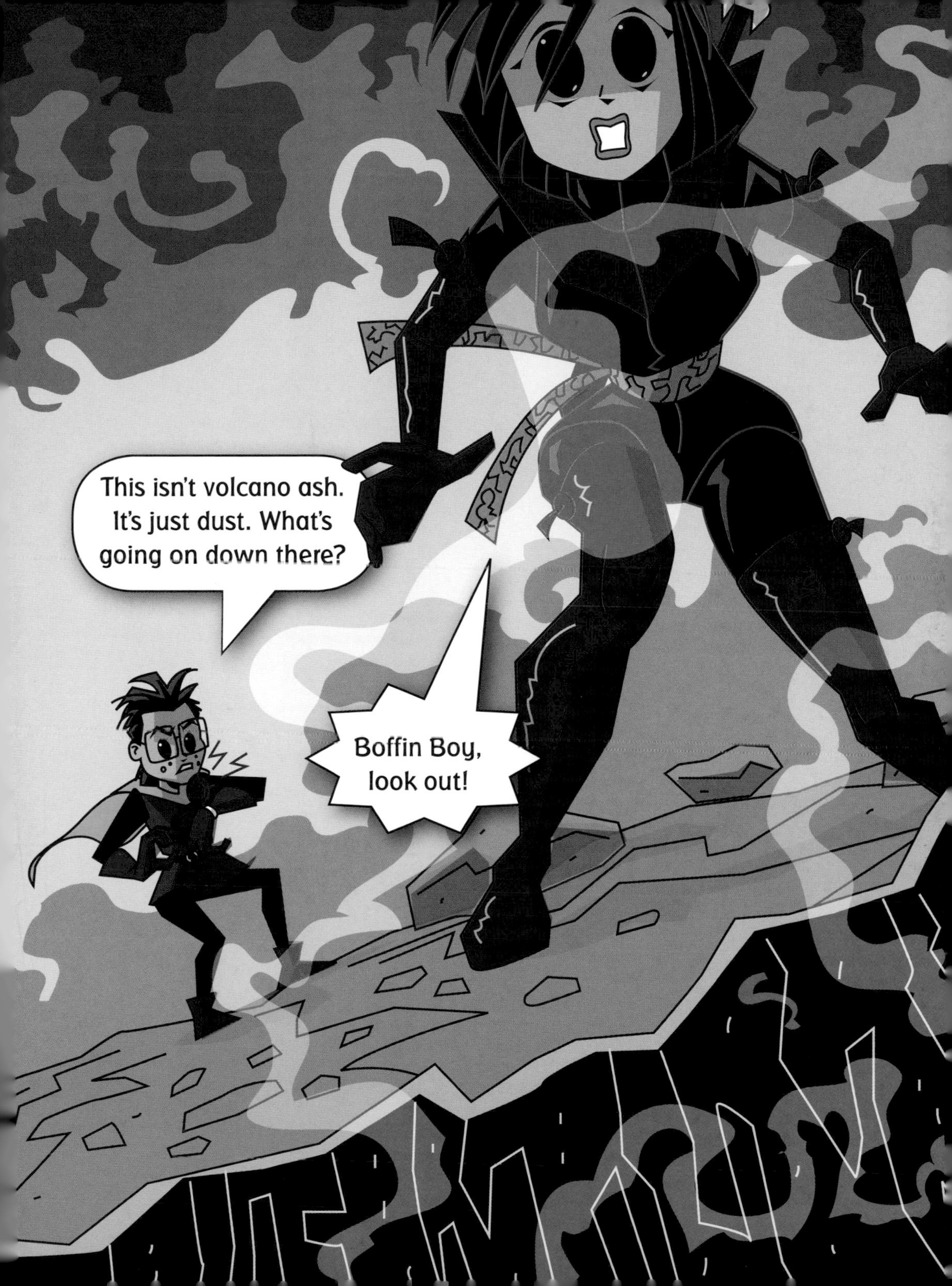
This isn't volcano ash. It's just dust. What's going on down there?
Boffin Boy, look out!

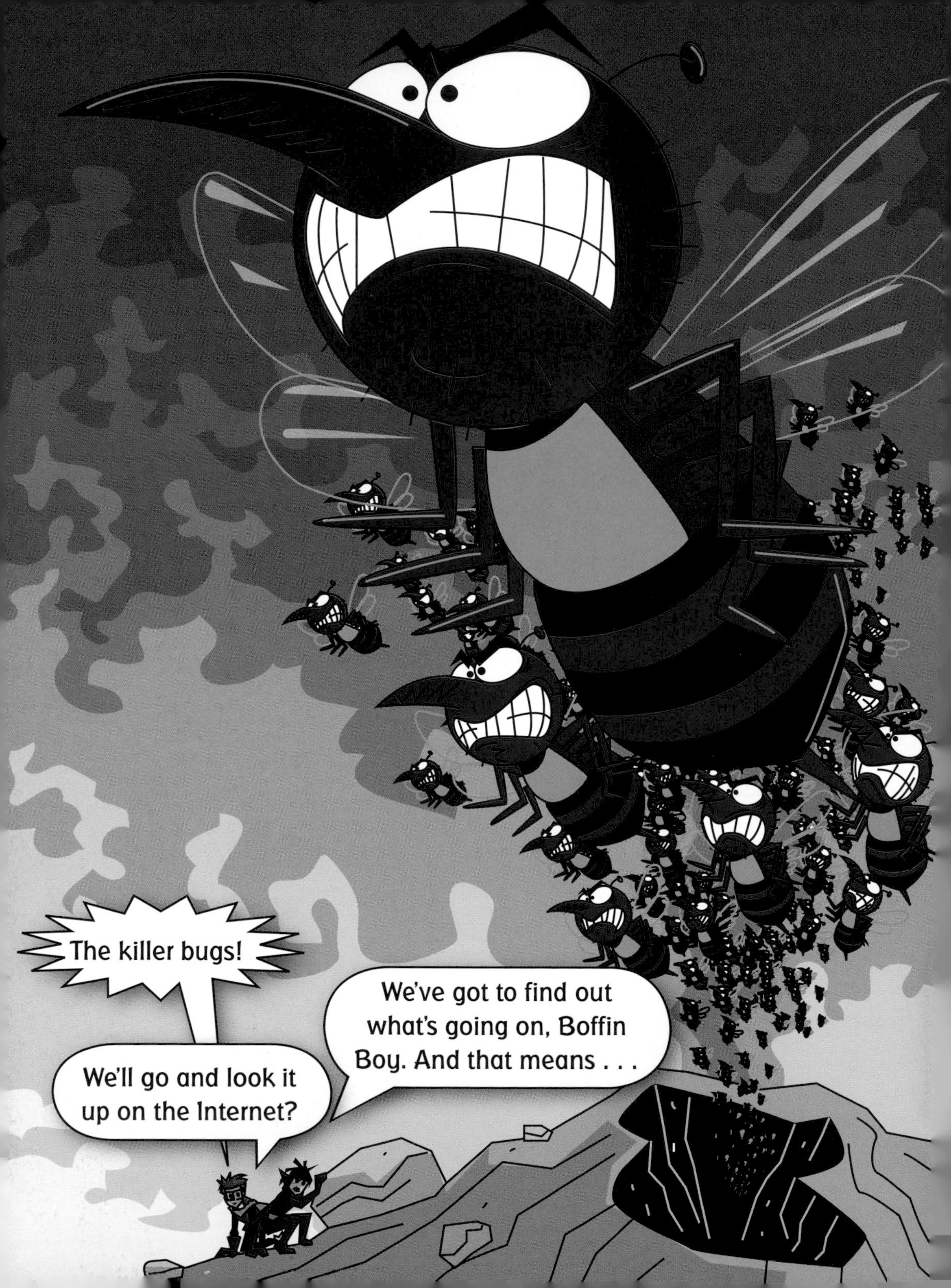
The killer bugs!
We'll go and look it up on the Internet?
We've got to find out what's going on, Boffin Boy. And that means . . .

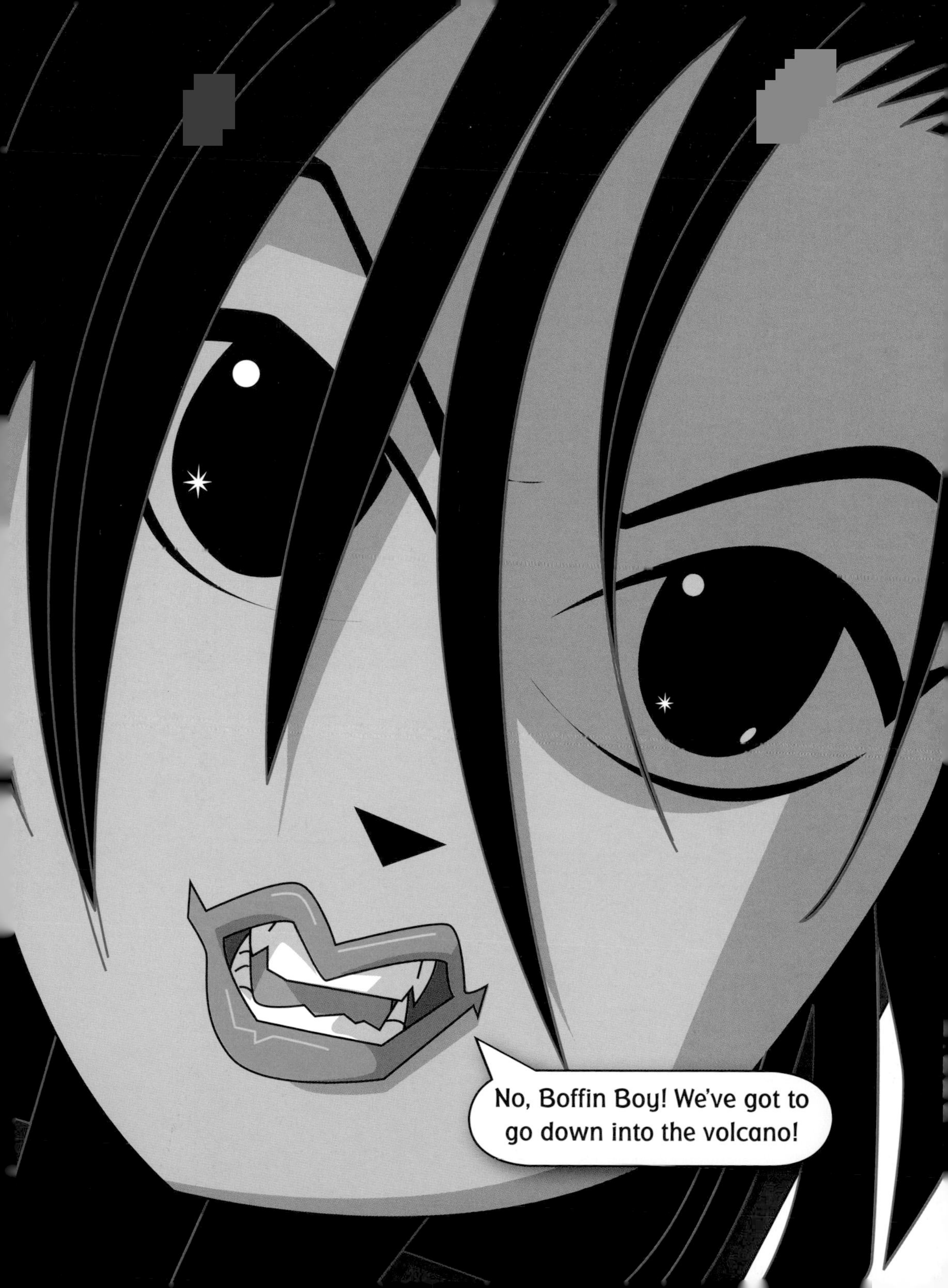
No, Boffin Boy! We've got to go down into the volcano!

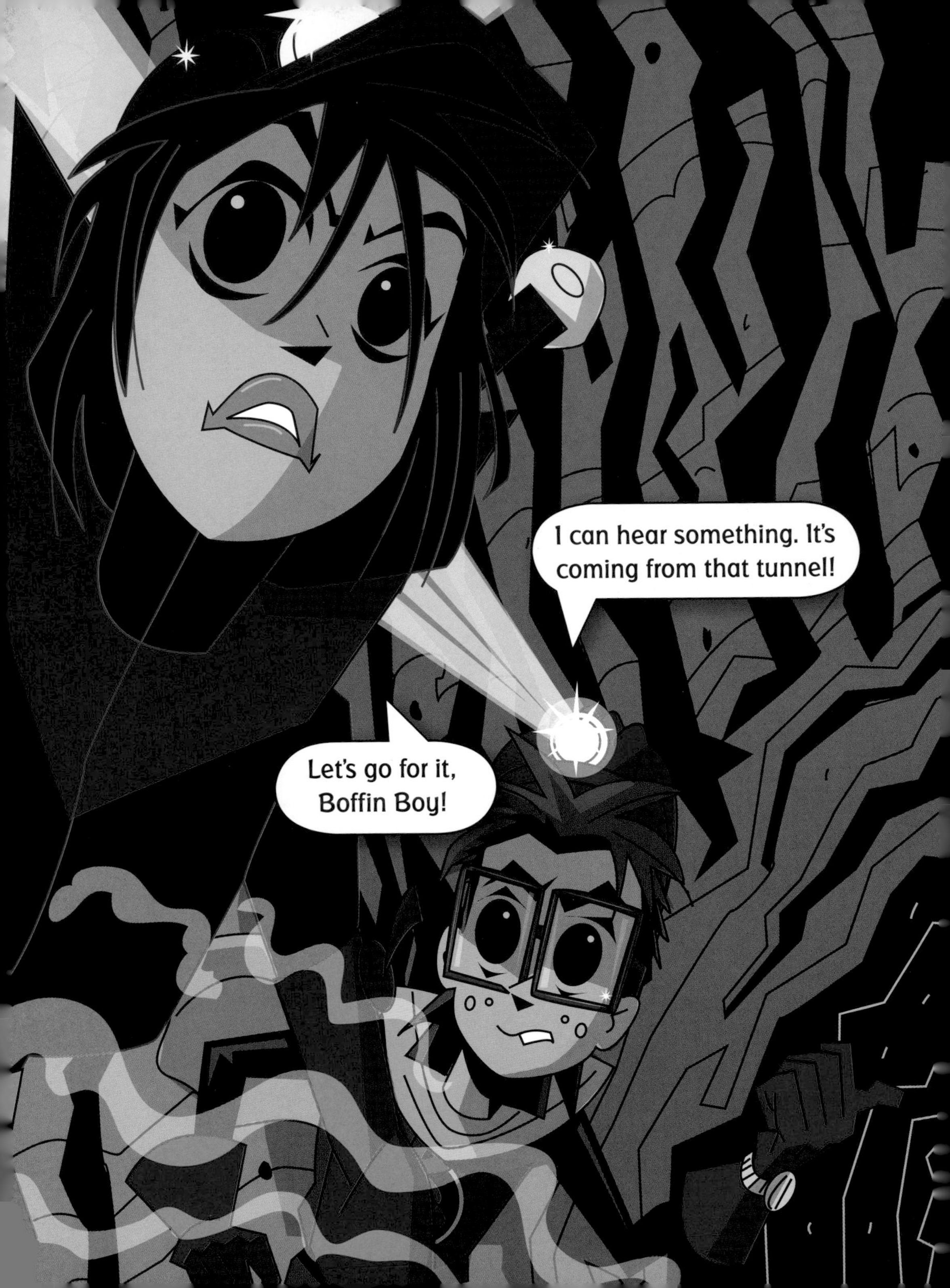
I can hear something. It's coming from that tunnel!
Let's go for it, Boffin Boy!

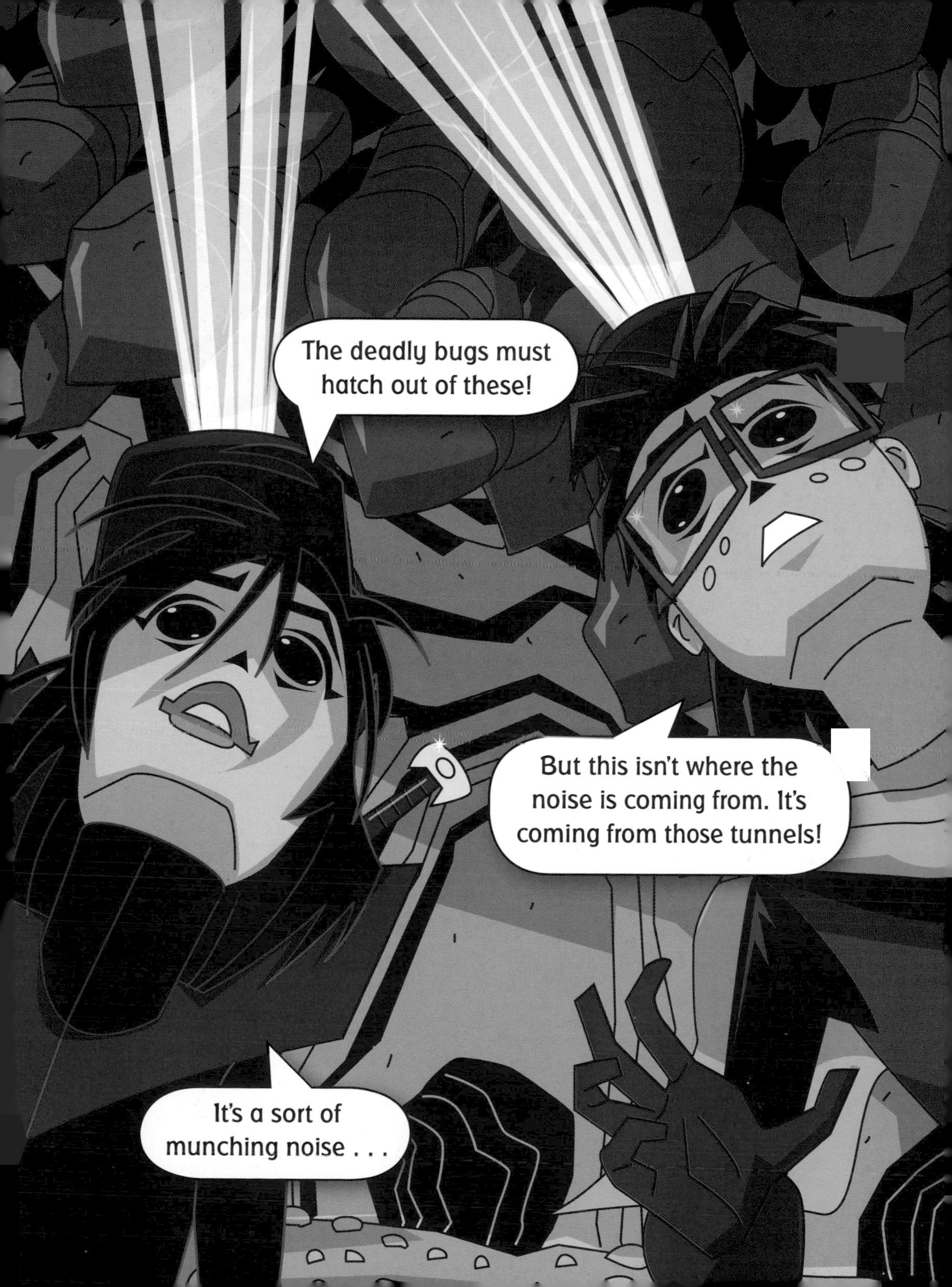
The deadly bugs must hatch out of these!
But this isn't where the noise is coming from. It's coming from those tunnels!
It's a sort of munching noise . . .

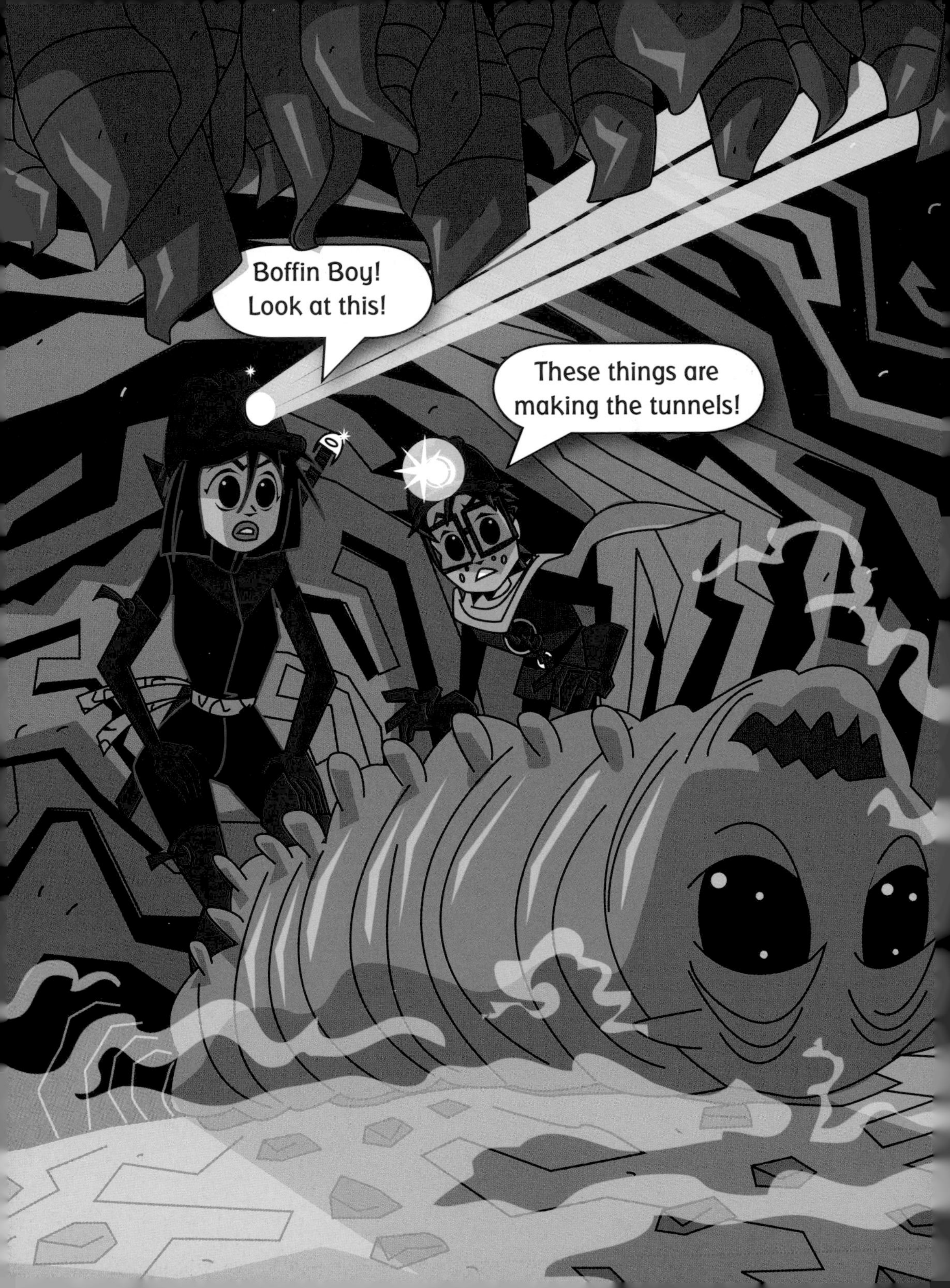
Boffin Boy! Look at this!
These things are making the tunnels!

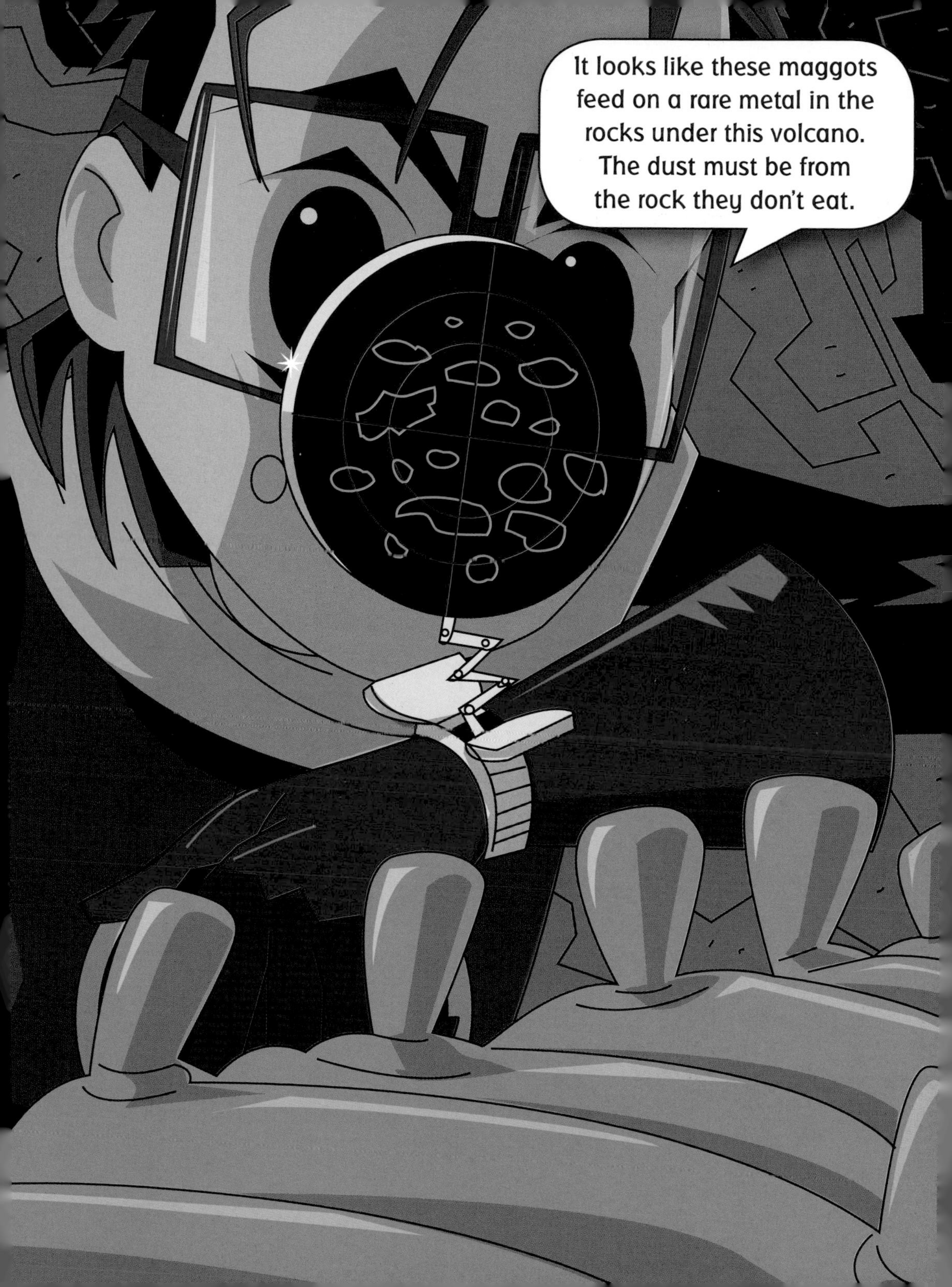
It looks like these maggots feed on a rare metal in the rocks under this volcano. The dust must be from the rock they don't eat.

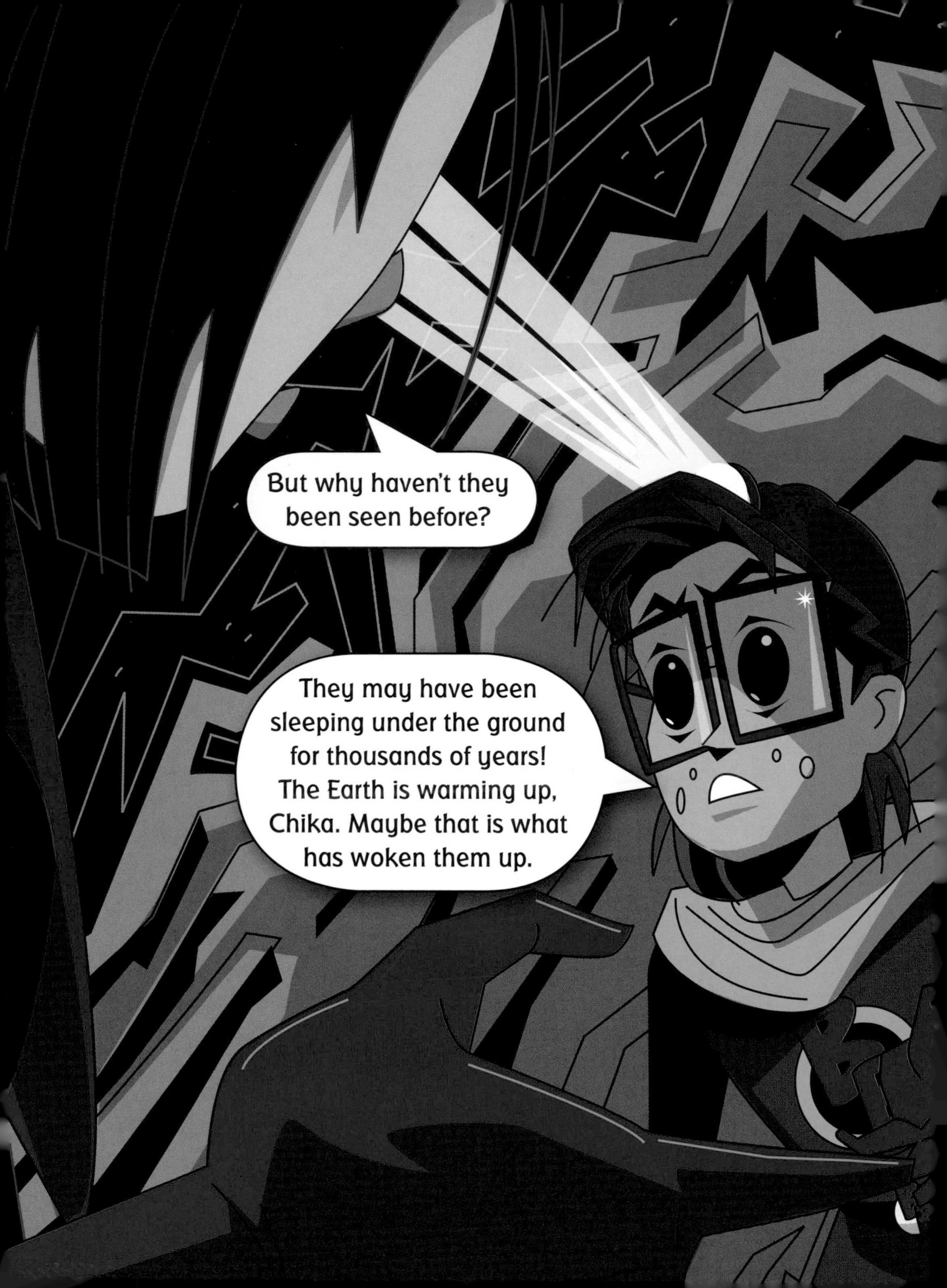
But why haven't they been seen before?
They may have been sleeping under the ground for thousands of years! The Earth is warming up, Chika. Maybe that is what has woken them up.

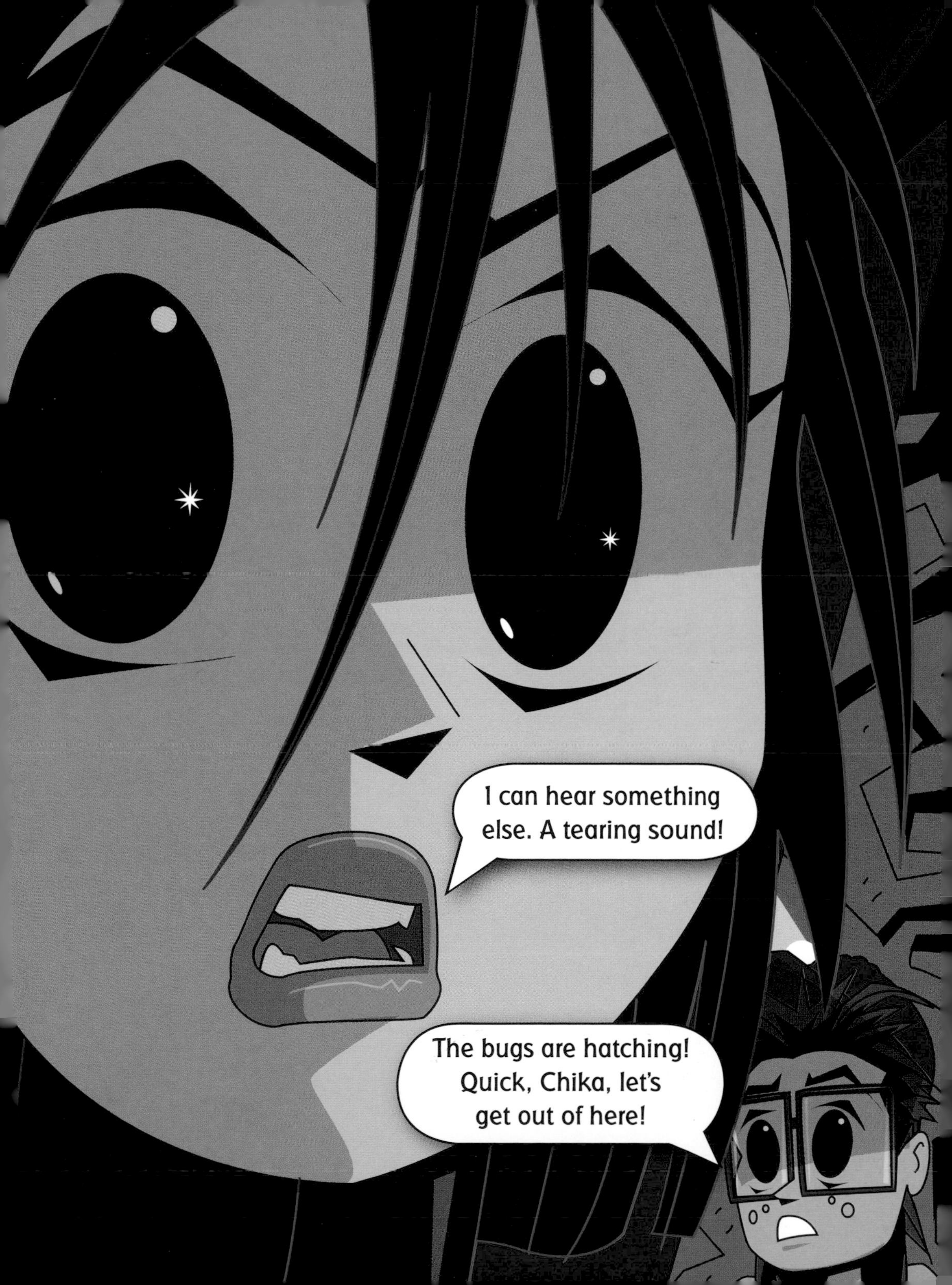
I can hear something else. A tearing sound!
The bugs are hatching! Quick, Chika, let's get out of here!

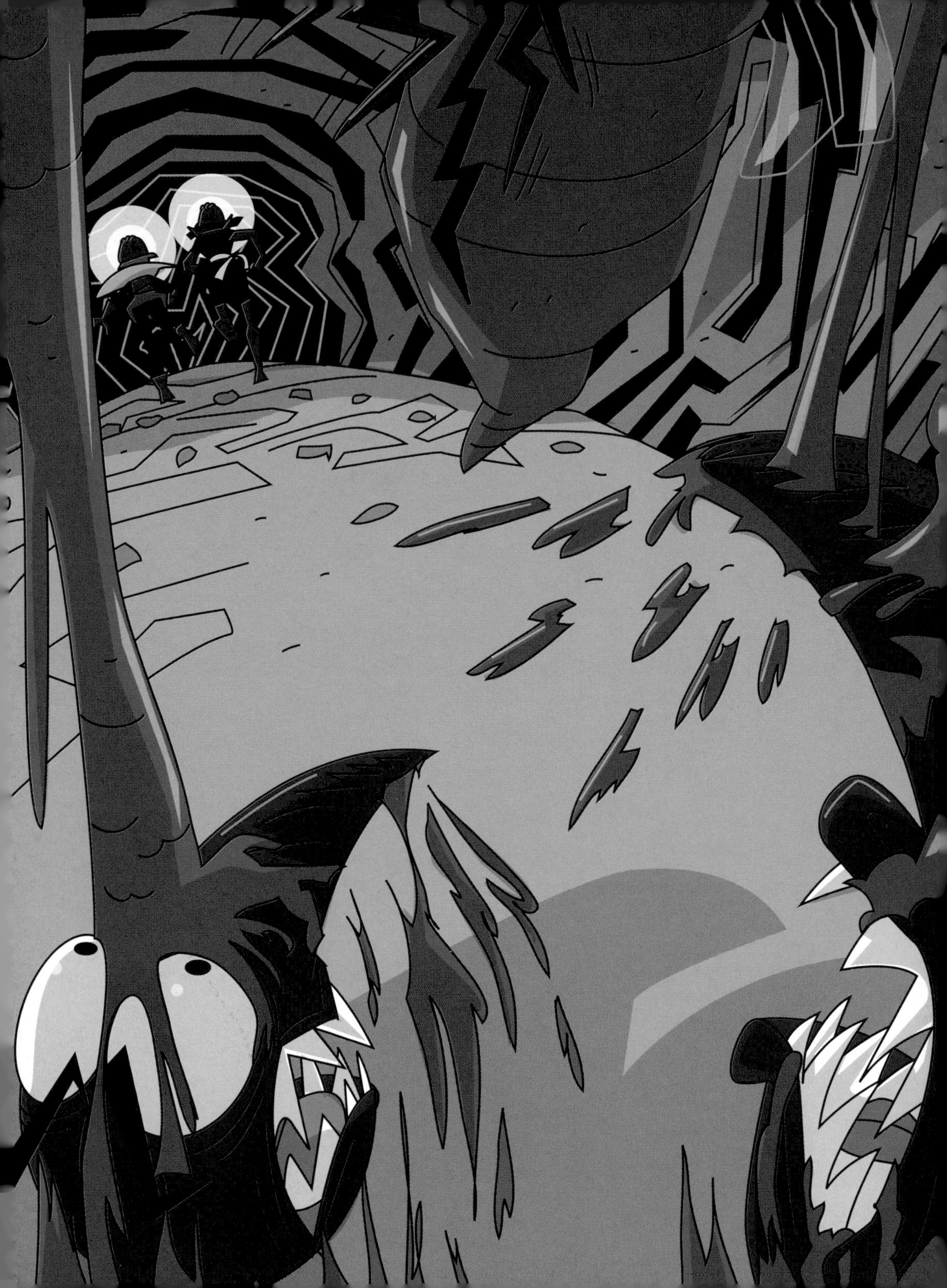

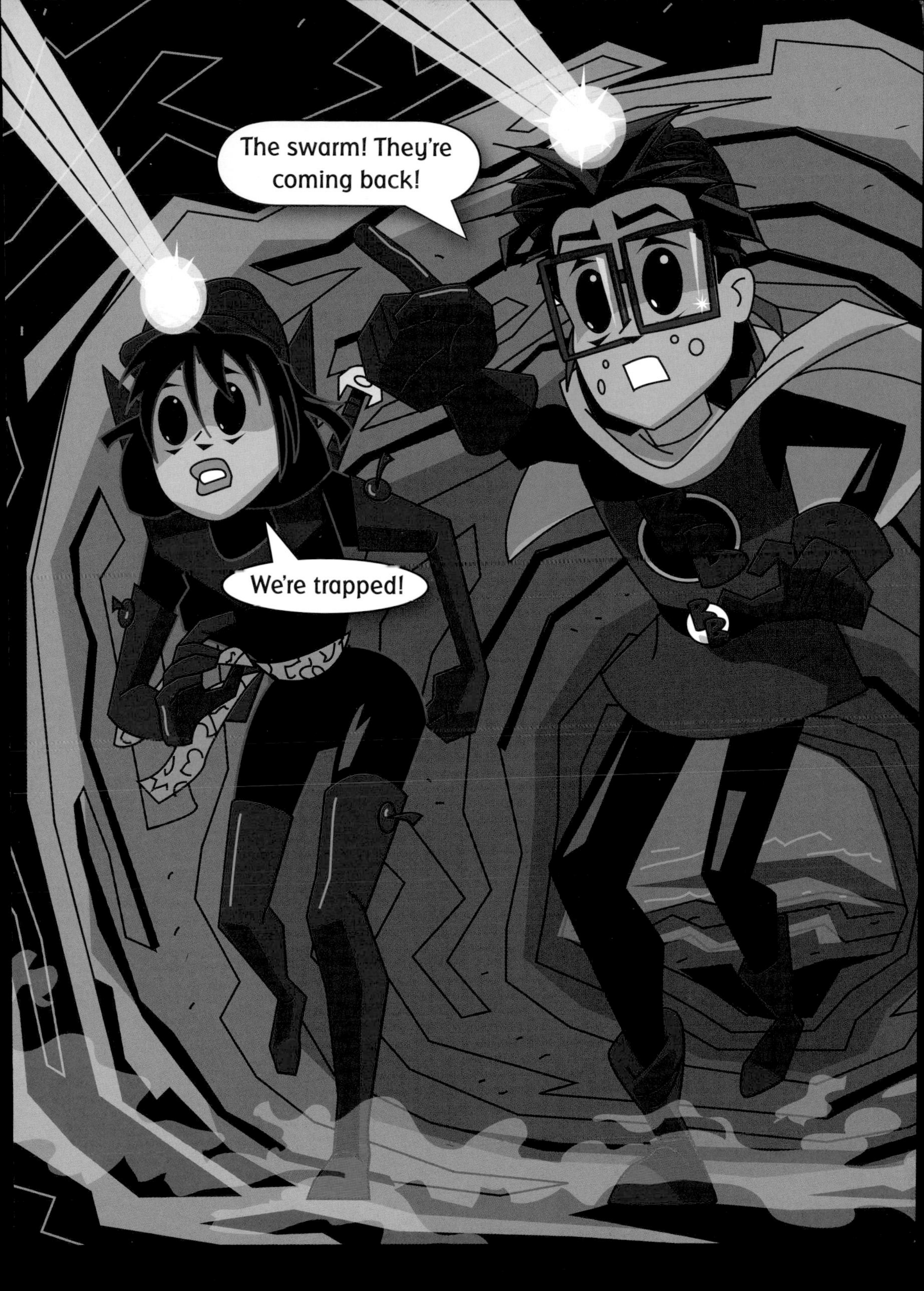
The swarm! They're coming back!
We're trapped!

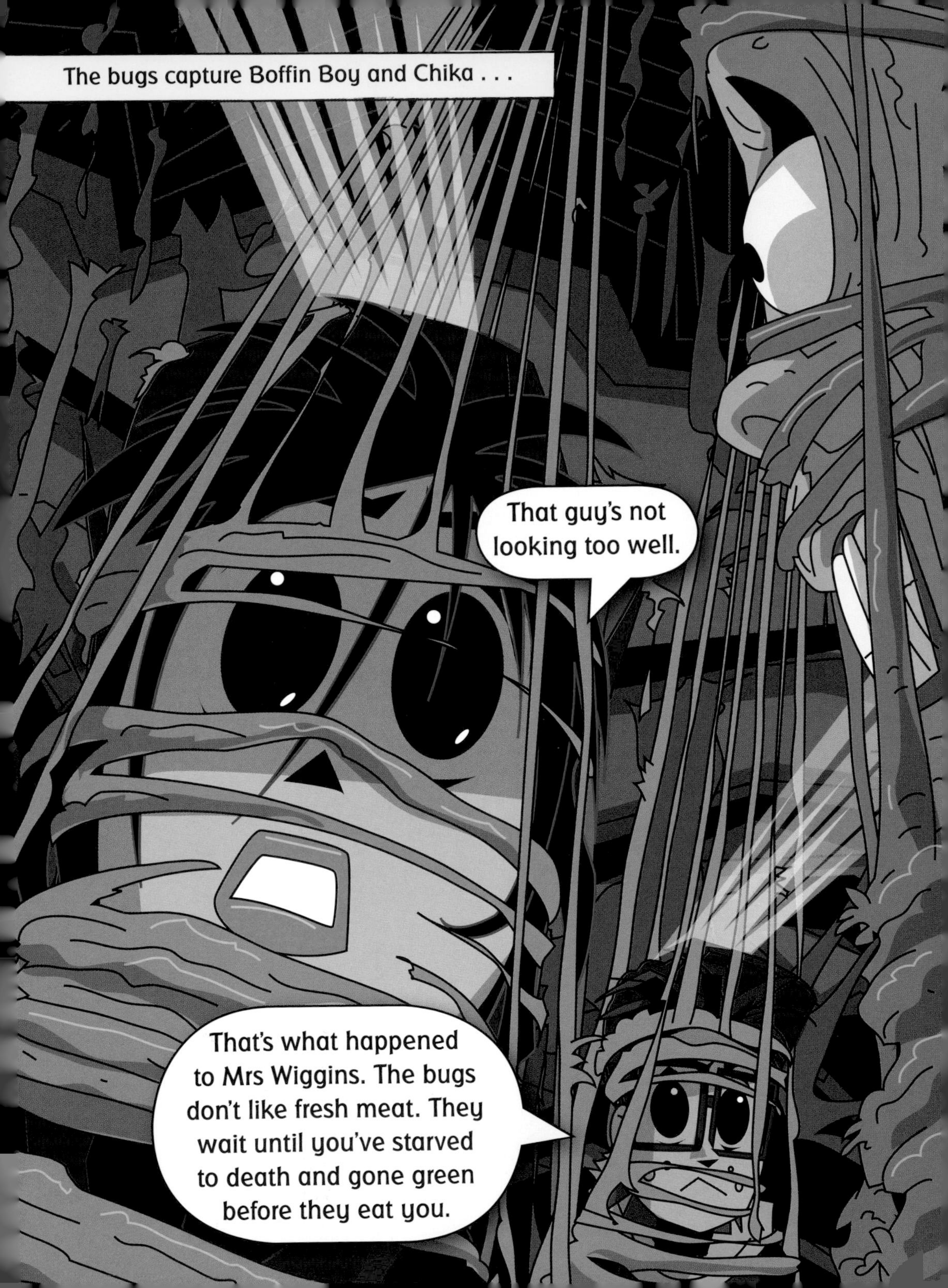
The bugs capture Boffin Boy and Chika . . .
That guy's not looking too well.
That's what happened to Mrs Wiggins. The bugs don't like fresh meat. They wait until you've starved to death and gone green before they eat you.

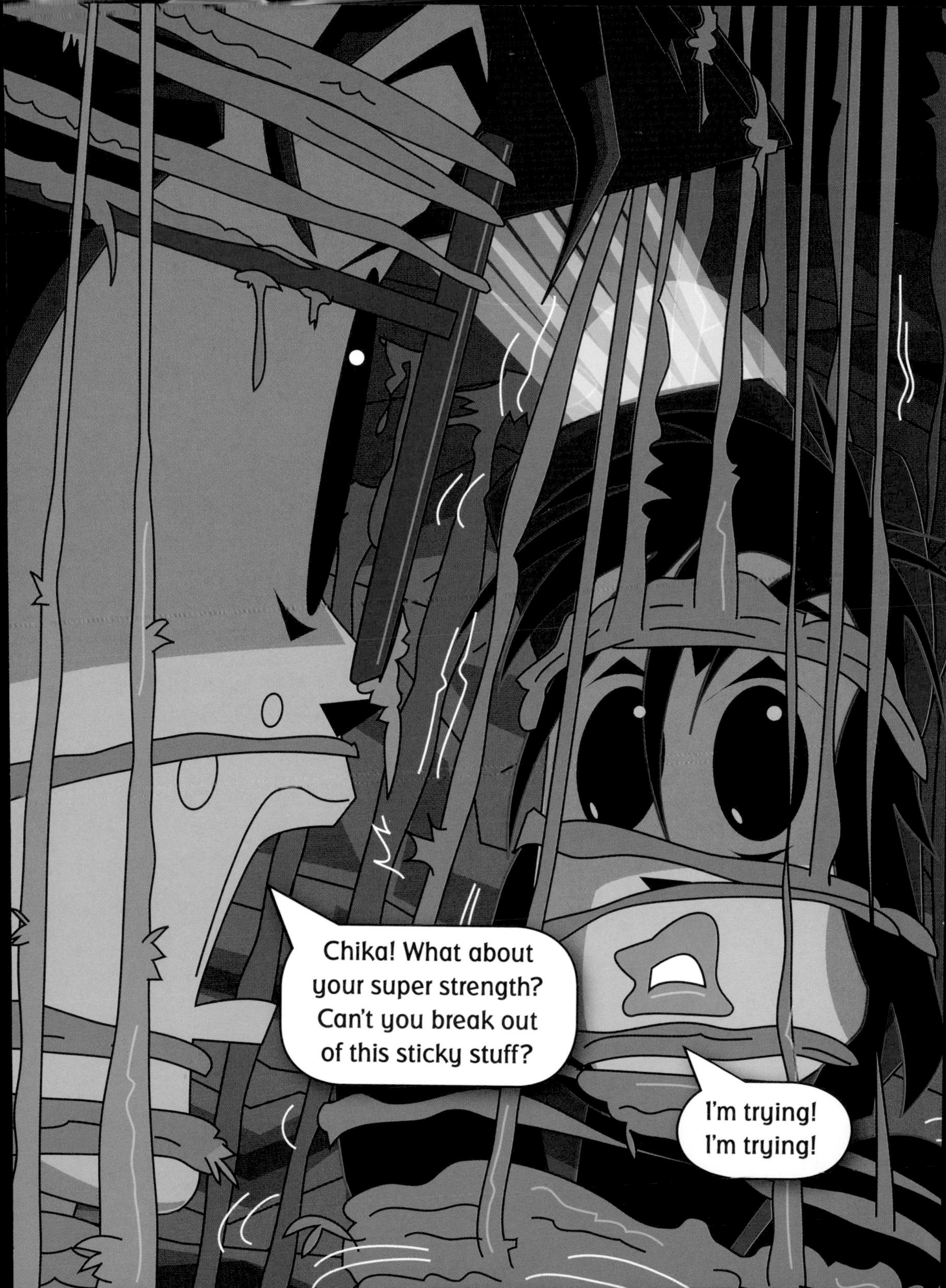
Chika! What about your super strength? Can't you break out of this sticky stuff?
I'm trying! I'm trying!

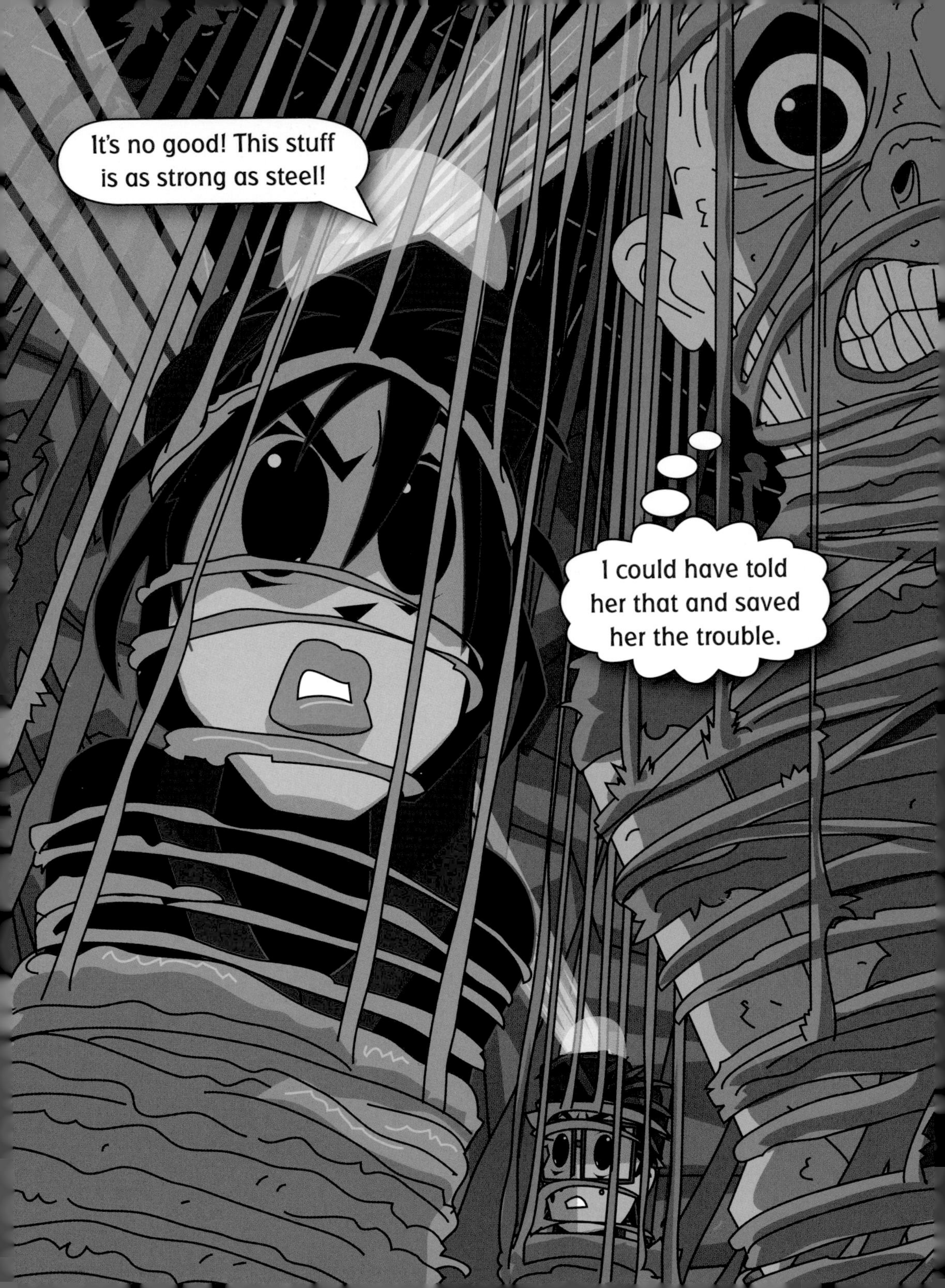
It's no good! This stuff is as strong as steel!
I could have told her that and saved her the trouble.

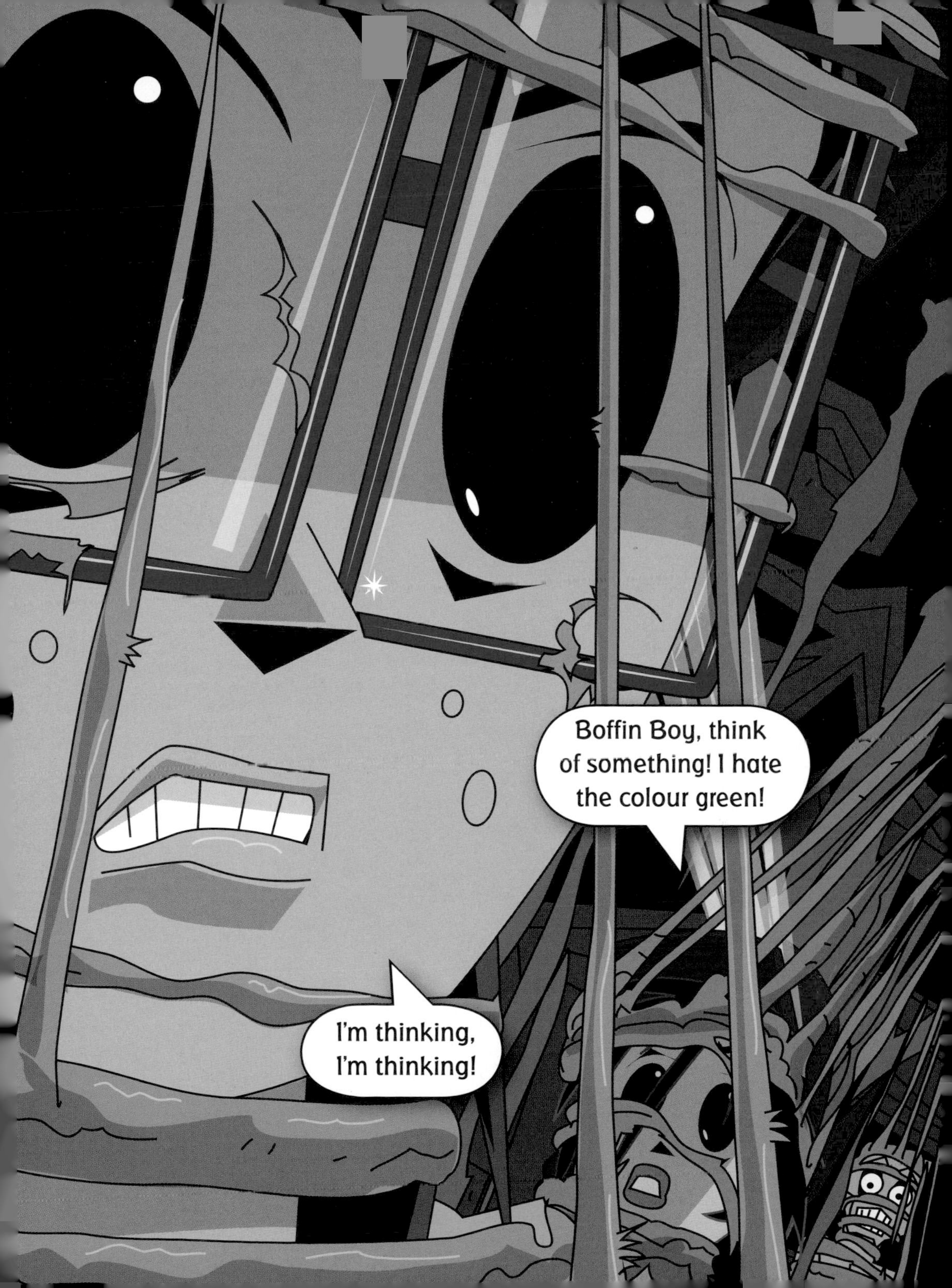
Boffin Boy, think of something! I hate the colour green!
I'm thinking, I'm thinking!

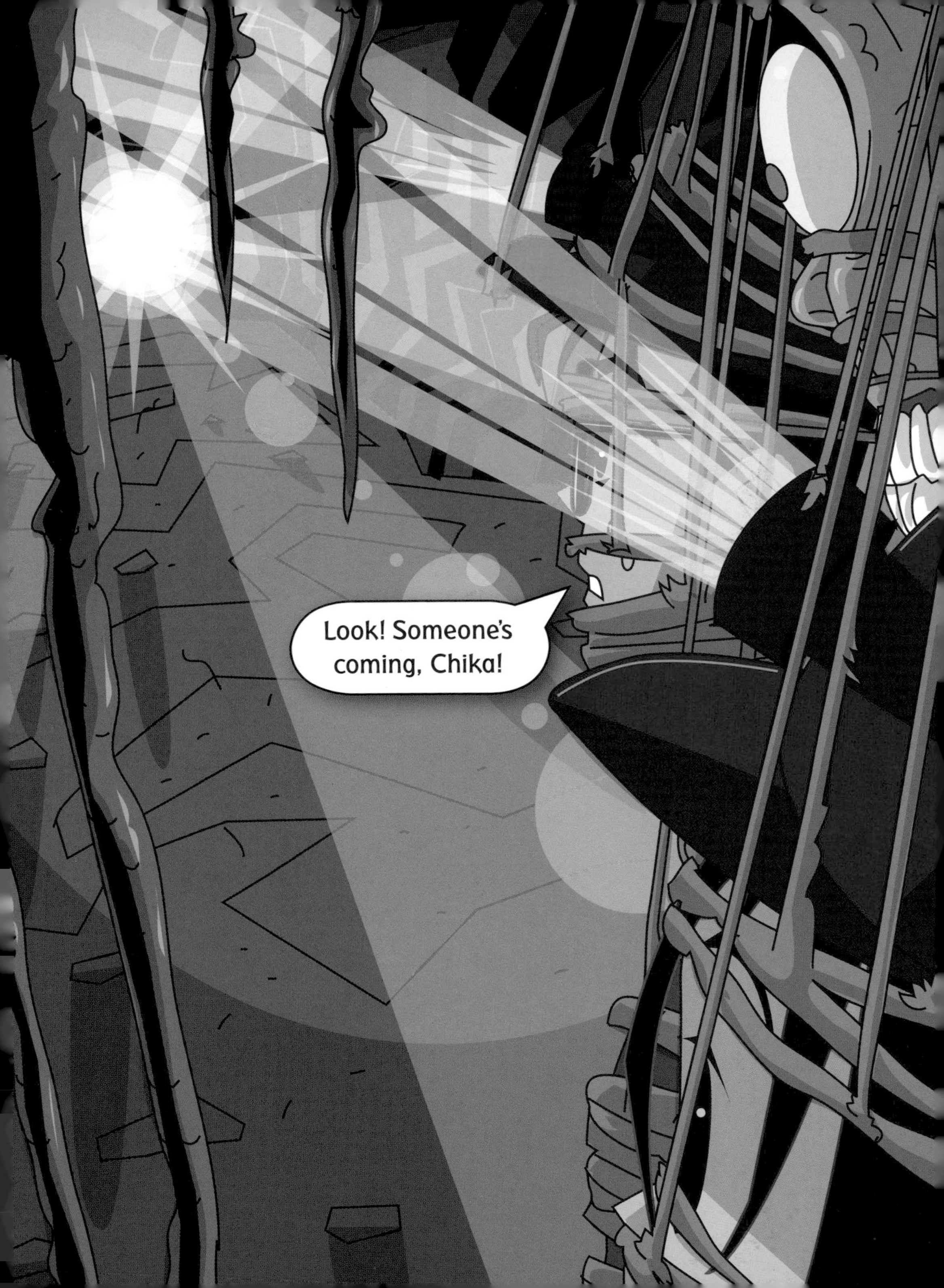
Look! Someone's coming, Chika!

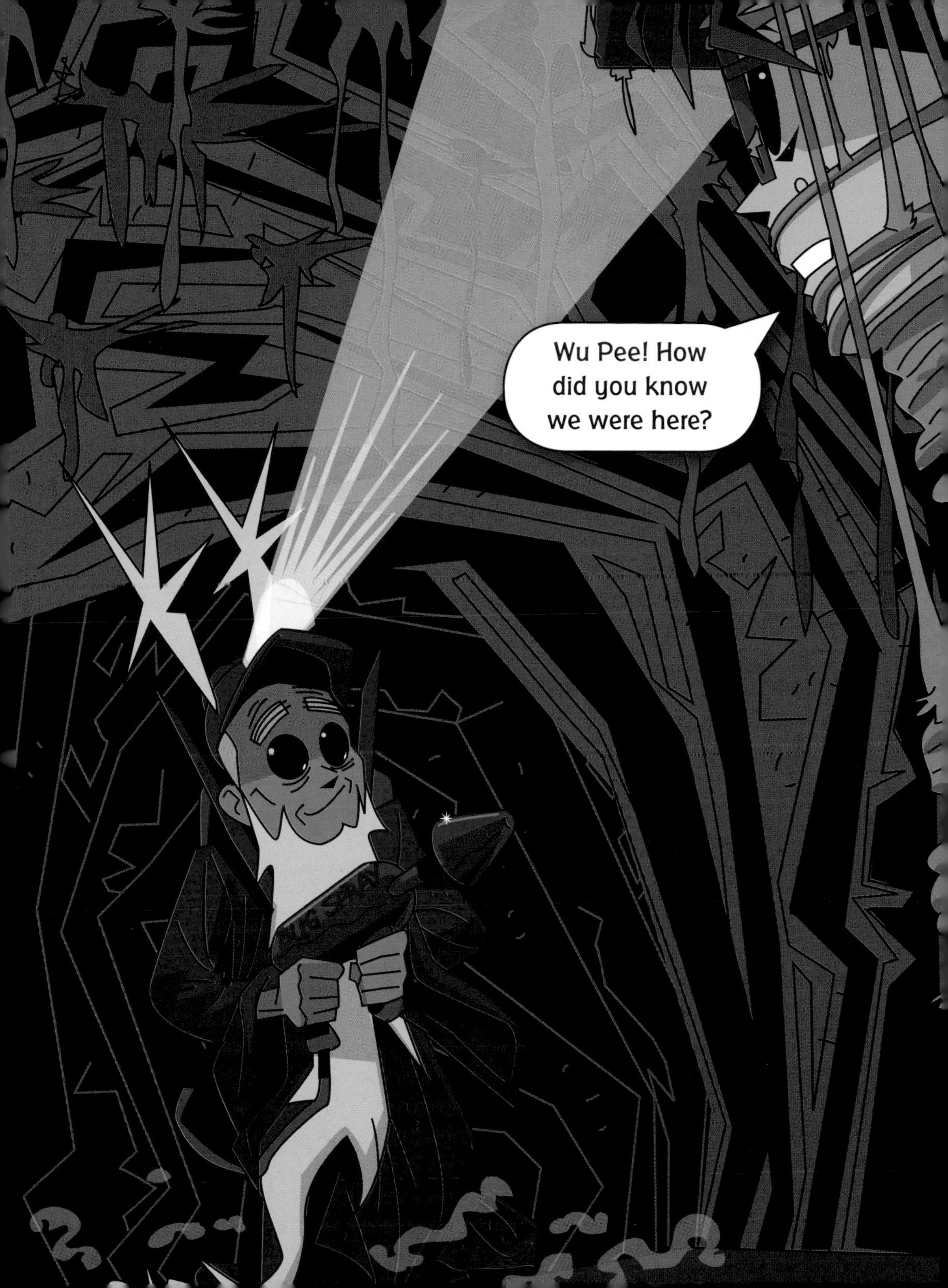
Wu Pee! How did you know we were here?

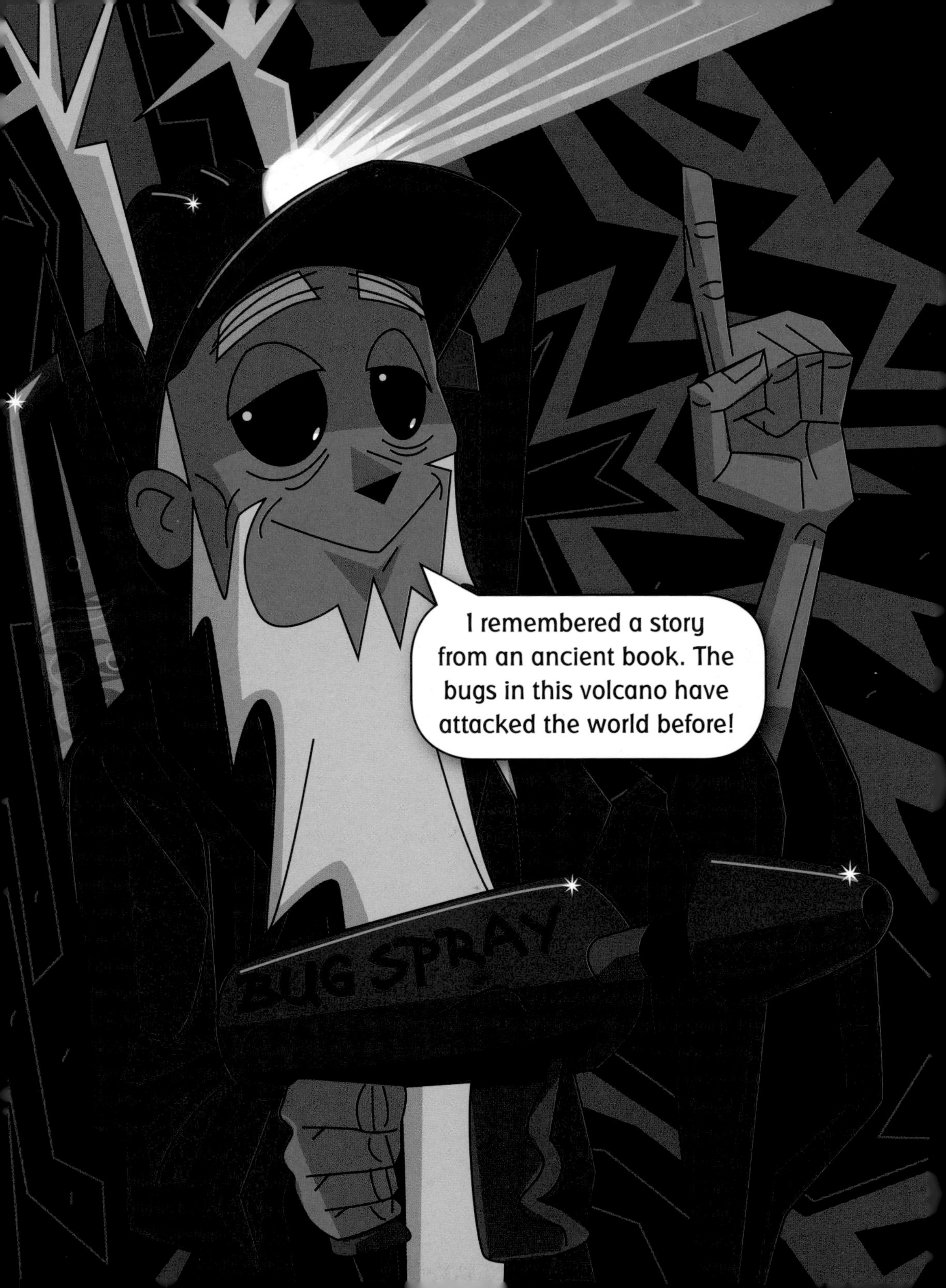
I remembered a story from an ancient book. The bugs in this volcano have attacked the world before!
BUG SPRAY

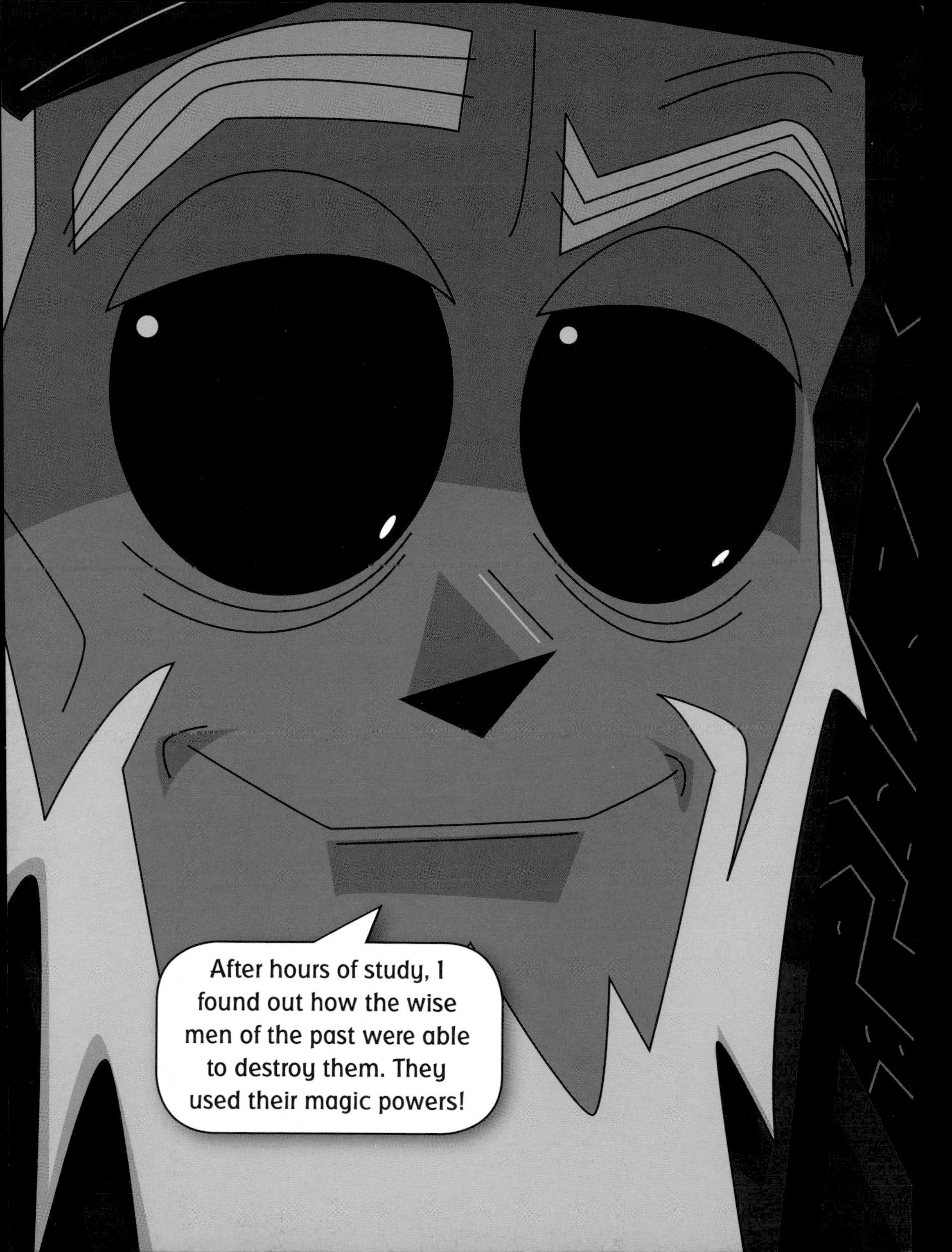
After hours of study, I found out how the wise men of the past were able to destroy them. They used their magic powers!

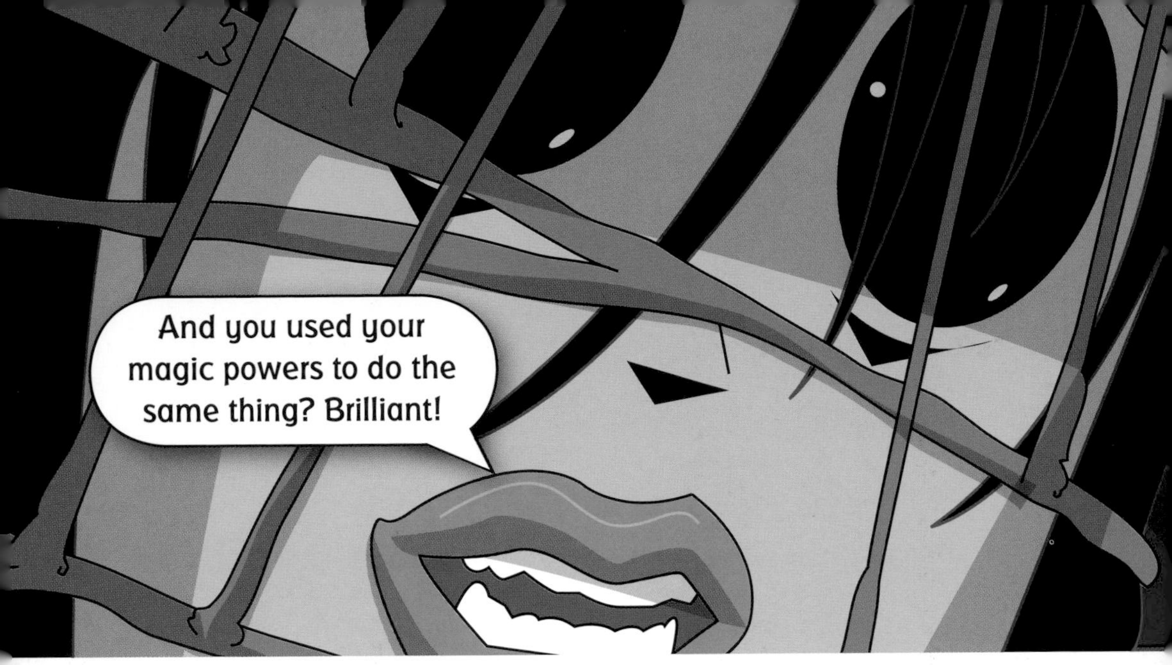
And you used your magic powers to do the same thing? Brilliant!

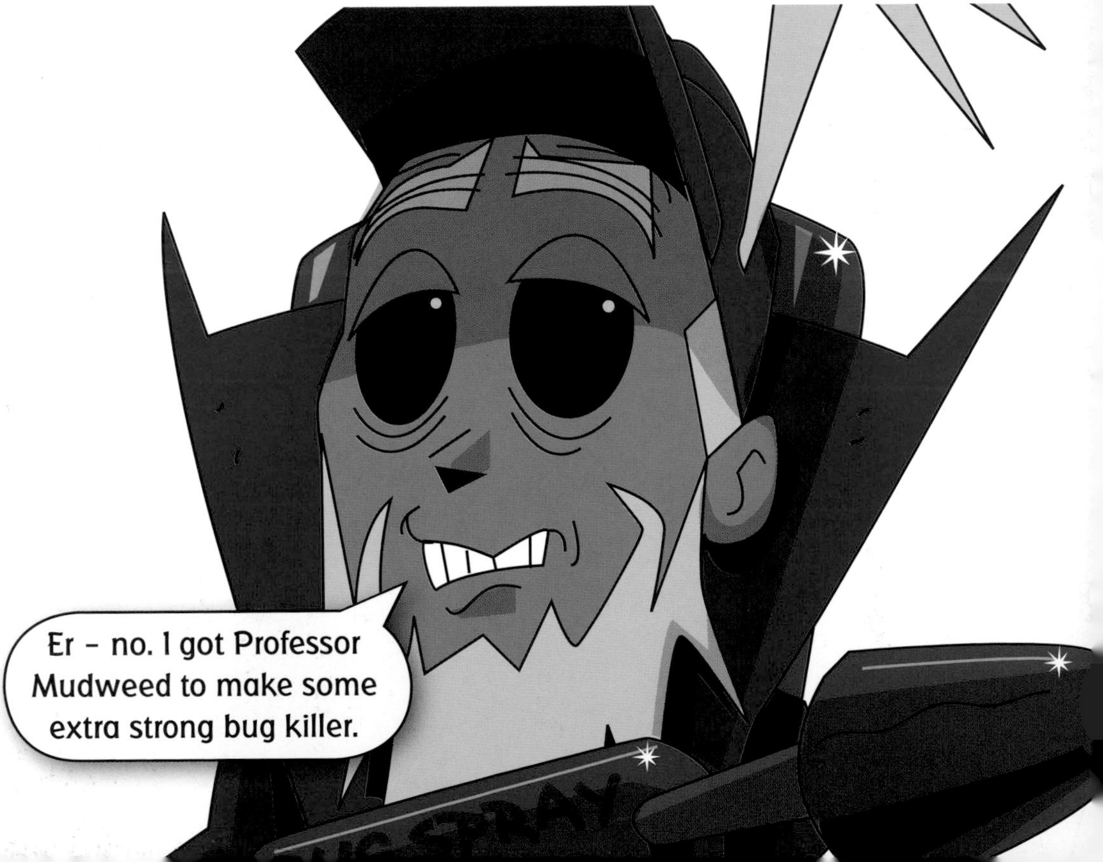
Er – no. I got Professor Mudweed to make some extra strong bug killer.

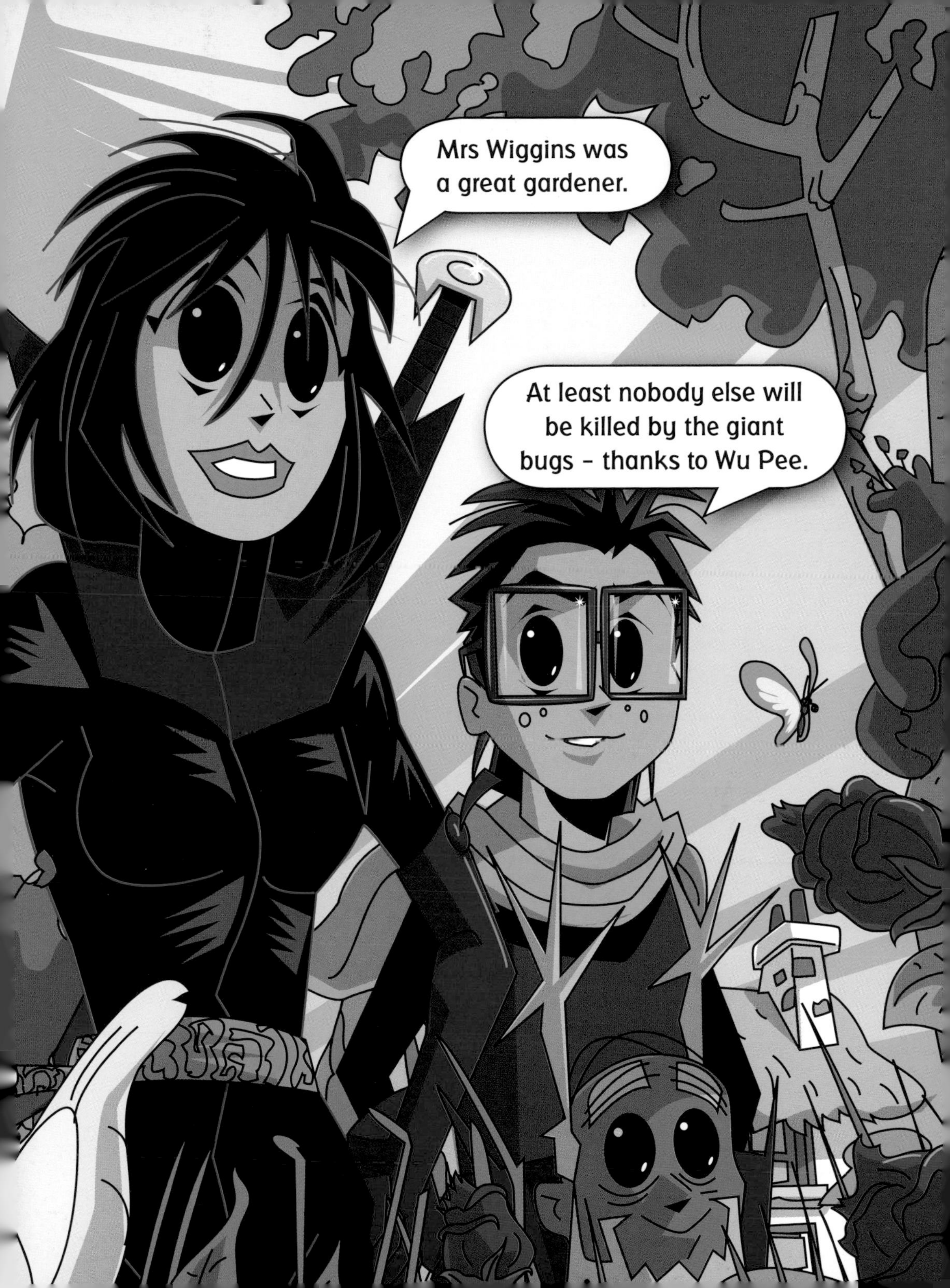
Mrs Wiggins was a great gardener.
At least nobody else will be killed by the giant bugs – thanks to Wu Pee.

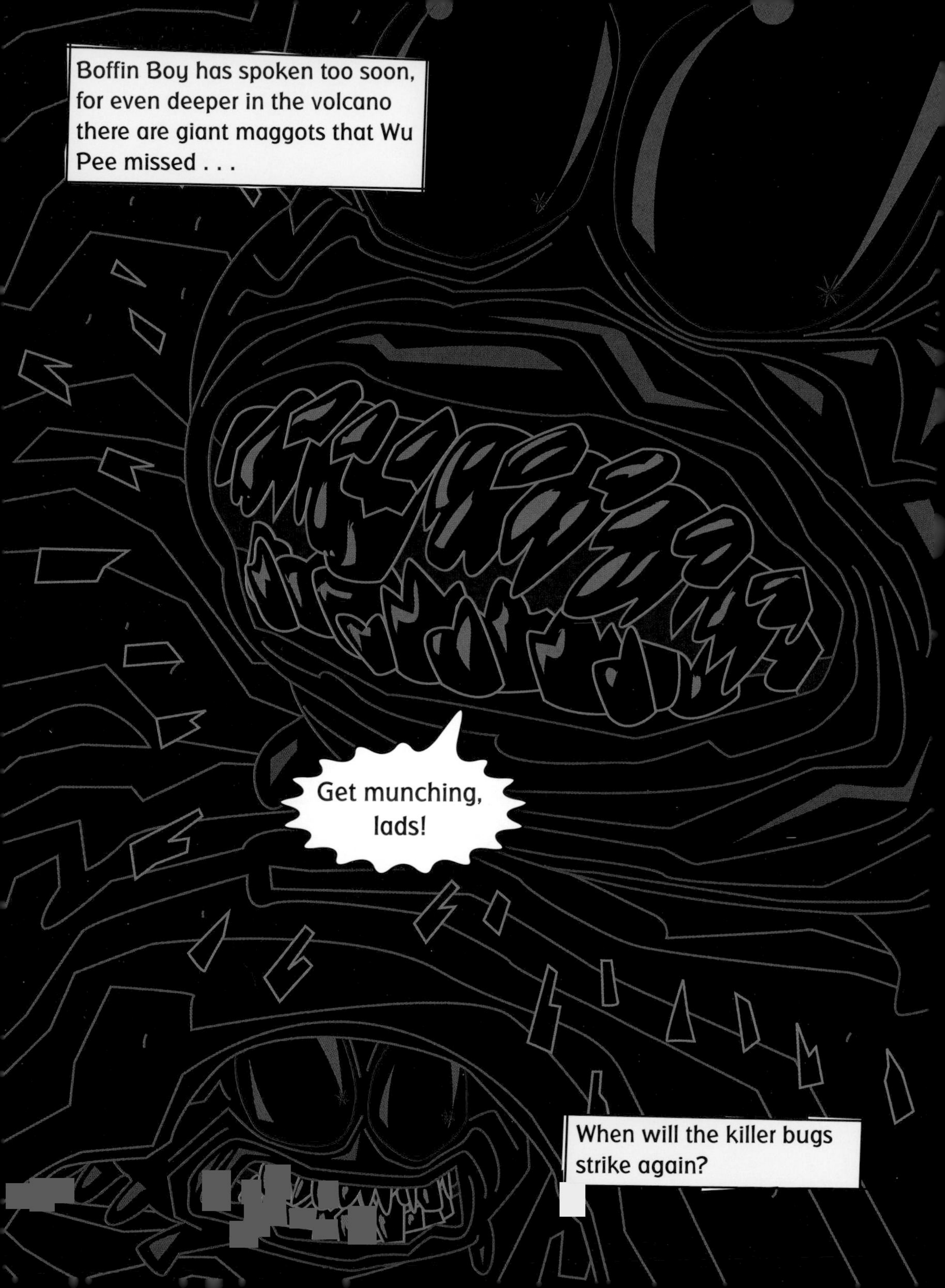
Boffin Boy has spoken too soon, for even deeper in the volcano there are giant maggots that Wu Pee missed . . .
Get munching, lads!
When will the killer bugs strike again?